THE GUNSMITH

#16

BUCKSKINS
AND
SIX-GUNS

Other Books
By
J.R. Roberts

Macklin's Women
The Chinese Gunmen
The Woman Hunt
The Guns of Abilene
Three Guns for Glory
Leadtown
The Longhorn War
Quanah's Revenge
Heavyweight Gun
New Orleans Fire
One-Handed Gun
The Canadian Payroll
Draw to an Inside Death
Dead Man's Hand
Bandit Gold
Buckskins and Six-Guns
Silver War
High Noon at Lancaster
Bandido Blood
Dodge City Gang
Sasquatch Hunt
Bullets and Ballots
Riverboat Gang

THE GUNSMITH

#16

BUCKSKINS
AND
SIX-GUNS

J.R. ROBERTS

SPEAKING VOLUMES, LLC
NAPLES, FLORIDA
2013

THE GUNSMITH
#16 BUCKSKINS AND SIX-GUNS

ISBN 978-1-61232-619-1

DEDICATION

For Anna,
who is the best at
everything she does.

Chapter One

Frank Leslie was a small wiry man who wore twin Colt Peacemakers on his hips, even while tending bar in the Buckskin Saloon. Leslie wore his hair long and flowing, with a mustache to match, and was constantly clad in buckskins, which is why he had come to be called Buckskin Frank Leslie.

Leslie had bought the saloon in Brightwater, Arizona in an effort finally to settle down. He had traveled most of his life, making his way with his guns, and had become weary of such a life. Here he hoped to make a home and be happy.

Now, eight months later, his dream seemed about to come apart. He was two months behind on his mortgage payments, and the bank manager was snapping at his heels, waiting to take the saloon over. He had been a fool, he realized, to believe that he could turn the saloon into a success in such a short time. If only he had the money to keep it going a little longer, he felt sure he would be able to make his payments on time. He had asked banker Sherman Jory for an extension but the man refused and was, in fact, anxious to foreclose and take over the business.

Buckskin Frank Leslie now had two more days in which to make his payments, or lose the Buckskin Saloon.

Martin Cort, who was Sherman Jory's "collector,"

entered the Buckskin Saloon and approached the bar. Leslie spotted him immediately and knew what was coming. Cort fancied himself a tough man, with and without a gun, and he delighted in pushing Buckskin Frank as far as he could. He knew of Leslie's reputation, but he did not know of Leslie's promise to himself to try and change the way he lived, which meant not being so free with his guns. Naturally, he still had to *wear* them. Not doing so was tantamount to suicide.

"Whiskey," Cort told Leslie.

"I don't serve you or your men, Cort," Leslie told him. "And that includes your boss."

"Is that a fact?" Cort asked. He was a big man, much larger than the wiry Leslie, but much as he would have liked to haul Leslie over that bar and beat him into the floor, he knew that his boss wouldn't take kindly to it—at least, not for two more days.

"In two days time, Leslie, me and my men are gonna be able to come in here and drink for nothing. What do you think about that?"

"I think you ought to come back in two days," Leslie replied. "At least then I might not be here to notice the stink."

Cort stiffened and his eyes narrowed. His right hand dropped to his gun and stopped there.

"I ought to kill you right now."

"Jory wouldn't like that at all, would he, Cort?" Leslie asked.

"In two days," Cort answered, "he won't care one way or the other."

"Like I said, then," Leslie answered, "come back in two days."

"Oh, I'll come back, Leslie," Cort said, pushing away from the bar, "I'll come back, and you better not be here when I do."

Leslie watched Cort walk out of the saloon and knew that sometime in the near future he would have to kill him—or be killed by him—just like old times.

All because of the Buckskin Saloon, which was supposed to change all of that.

Martin Cort was quivering as he left the saloon and brushed by a man who was on his way in.

"Watch where you're going," Cort growled and kept going. The man called something after him, but Cort didn't hear it.

He wanted the go-ahead to kill Buckskin Frank Leslie, and he was going to talk to his boss about it. Not only did he dislike Leslie, but killing him would enhance his own reputation. Buckskin Frank Leslie was not quite as well-known a name as Bill Hickok, but Hickok was dead and out of reach, and Leslie was close at hand and ready to be taken. All Cort needed was the word.

The man with the word was sitting in his office at the Bank of Brightwater, wishing he were at Kelly's House of Leisure instead, a whorehouse of which he owned a large part. He had obtained that piece of property in the same manner he was intending to obtain the Buckskin Saloon—by foreclosure.

Sherman Jory had the idea of using his position as bank manager to own more than half of the town's businesses eventually, and the only reason he was willing to settle for that was that—in his own estimation—he was not a greedy enough man.

Which might have been his only flaw.

There was a knock at his office door and his secretary—a lovely little thing whom he would much rather have had working for him at Kelly's—entered and told him that Martin Cort was asking to see him.

"Send him in." Although he usually referred to Martin Cort as his "executive assistant," Cort was actually his chief henchman, his collector, and he thought he knew what the man wanted to talk to him about.

When Cort entered Jory said, "Sit down, Martin."

"Mr. Jory—"

"Just sit down," Jory said. "I believe I know why you're here."

"You do?" Cort asked. It annoyed him that he was afraid of Sherman Jory. The banker was older, smaller and no match for Cort, but he still wielded a lot of power in town. He looked the part. He had white hair and a bushy white beard, and he always wore three-piece suits. Expensive rings adorned fingers on each hand and he waved them about for all to see when he spoke.

He waved them now as he said, "You went to see Frank Leslie again, didn't you?"

"Well, I—sure, but only to, uh, remind him—"

"I'm going to tell you this just one more time, Martin," Jory said, laying both of his palms on his desk top. "You see only who I tell you to see."

"What about my private life?"

"Your private life does not include Frank Leslie," Jory replied. "As a matter of fact, I don't think you should have a private life while you're working for me. You want to get laid, you go to Kelly's. You want to play poker or drink, you go to the Brightwater Saloon to do it. That is, unless you don't want to work for me anymore, Martin?"

The older man's eyes stared coldly into Cort's, and Cort felt himself go cold all over.

"No, sir, I don't want to stop working for you."

"Then remember to stay away from Frank Leslie," Jory advised him.

"For two more days."

"Until I say so." Jory shook his head and chuckled saying, "I don't know why you're so anxious to pit your gun against that of Buckskin Frank Leslie, Cort. Do you have a suicide wish?"

"I can take Leslie," Cort insisted.

"Well, maybe you'll find out," Jory said, "but not until I say so. Understood?"

"Understood," Martin replied sullenly.

"Then get out. I have work to do."

Cort glared at his employer, then got up and walked from the office. Outside he stopped by the desk where Jory's secretary, Jesse Wells, was sitting, but she pointedly ignored him. She'd come around, he thought. The bitch, she'd come around when he had enough money, which was another reason he took Sherman Jory's abuse. The man paid him well, and he saved his money.

Bitch, he thought again, and left the bank.

Jesse Wells watched Martin Cort walk out and shuddered. She loathed the man, and feared him. She wished she had a man of her own, a good man, who would keep Cort away from her.

In his office, Sherman Jory took out the agreement that Frank Leslie had signed when he was loaned the money to pay for the Buckskin Saloon. Two more days, he thought, two more days and he would own another business in Brightwater.

He'd be another step closer to being the most powerful man in Brightwater, and maybe, after that, Arizona.

Chapter Two

The Gunsmith entered Brightwater with the intention of making it his last stop before leaving Arizona and heading on into Nevada.

He reined in his team and stopped his rig right in front of the Buckskin as soon as he spotted it. Quenching his thirst was the uppermost thing in his mind at that moment, after which he'd tend to his animals and then go looking for a room and a bath.

He dropped down to the ground and walked around behind the rig to where his big black gelding, Duke, stood.

"Just one drink, big boy," he said, "and then I'll take you to the livery. I can't remember the last time I was this thirsty."

Duke gave him a baleful stare and the Gunsmith decided to take that as a look of understanding. He patted the big fella's neck and stepped up onto the boardwalk. As he approached the batwing doors to the saloon a man came barreling out and brushed past him roughly.

"Watch where you're going."

"Good advice, mister," Clint called after him, but the man just kept on walking and Clint decided not to pursue the matter. He entered the saloon and approached the bar.

"What can I get you?" the bartender asked him, but this barkeep was like no other Clint Adams had ever seen. A thin, not very tall fella with long hair and a long mustache, he was the first bartender Clint had ever seen who wore two Colt Peacemakers on his hips. And was also clad in buckskins, which struck a familiar note in the back of Clint's mind. . . .

"A beer," he answered the man, "and preferably a cold one."

"Coming up."

When the bartender brought his beer Clint noticed something else odd about the man, considering his profession, and that was that he didn't talk much. He just set the beer down and moved to another part of the bar. Odd thing for a bartender to do, considering Clint was a stranger in town, but it suited him since he didn't feel much like talking either.

It was early and there were only one or two other customers in the saloon; Clint was the only one at the bar. He drank down half of his beer in one swallow, washing the traildust out of his mouth and throat, then took his time over the other half. He was just finishing it up when four men entered the saloon together, visible to him through the mirror behind the bar.

They were dressed in trail clothes covered with dust, indicating they'd been riding for some time. Three of them wore tied-down Colts on their right hips, and one wore a similar gun on his left. From the size and shape of them, it didn't take a genius to figure out that they were kin to each other, probably brothers.

The four moved en masse to the other end of the bar and ordered a bottle of whiskey and four glasses.

Peripherally aware that he was being watched, Clint dropped a coin on the bar for the beer and headed for the door. When one of the four men called out to him, he wasn't really surprised. You get so you can smell trouble, and he'd caught a good whiff of it when the men had entered.

"Adams," one of them called, and he stopped.

"How do you know my name?" he asked with his back to them.

"We been trailing you since Yuma, Adams," the same man answered. "Me and my brothers was sorry we missed you there."

"Do you have some business with me?"

"We do," the man said, "and if you'll turn around we can get right to it."

"I don't know you men—" Clint started to say, but the other man cut him off.

"We're the Banners," the man said, "and we're gonna kill you."

"I'll say it again," Clint repeated. "I don't know you men, and I have no quarrel with you."

"Quarrel don't enter into this," the man said. "You're the Gunsmith, Adams, so you been up against it before."

Reputation seekers, he knew, and yes, he'd been up against it before. Too many times before. He'd been outnumbered before, too, but four to one was a little more than he cared for.

"If I turn around," he explained, "you men know that at least two of you will die, maybe more."

"We talked it over," the voice answered, "and even if only one of us is left standing, at least he'll have your reputation."

The Gunsmith finally turned around and stared at the four men in wonder.

"Are you men brothers?"

"We are," the same man answered. He appeared to be the oldest.

"And my reputation is worth the life of three of you?

To one of you it's worth the lives of your brothers?''

Clint pinned his eyes on the youngest of four, who seemed to fidget beneath his stare, but it was still the eldest who spoke.

"We agreed," he said. "We heard you was in Yuma, but you was gone when we got there. We rode a long way to get here, and now that we found you we ain't gonna change our mind. Boys," he said to his brothers, and they fanned out across the saloon floor. The other two customers got up from their tables and left in a hurry, leaving only the Banners, the Gunsmith—and the bartender.

"Hold on," Clint heard the bartender say. He looked over and saw the buckskin-clad man come out from behind the bar.

"Keep out of this, bartender," the oldest brother said, without taking his eyes off the Gunsmith. "It's none of your business."

"This is my place, Banner, and that makes it my business," the man said. "But even if you move it out to the street, I can't stand by and watch four men draw on one."

"The Gunsmith don't need no help," Banner said.

"Any man needs help when he's facing four guns," the bartender said. He moved along the bar until he was standing a couple of feet from Clint, facing the four Banner brothers.

"You siding with him?" Banner asked, frowning at the man with the buckskins and six-guns. "Are you crazy?" Banner asked when the bartender nodded his head.

"Are you ready to die?" the other man shot back.

"The odds are still in our favor," Banner insisted.

"You men can walk out of here right now," Clint said, "with no hard feelings."

The older Banner brother shook his head slowly and said, "No way. We've come too far."

"Does your brother speak for all of you?" Clint asked. When the other men exchanged glances, but did not speak, Clint said, "If he does, then I'm sorry."

"You can't talk us out of this, Adams," Banner said.

"What happens next is up to you, Banner."

What happened next was that Banner went for his gun and a split second behind him were his three brothers. Unfortunately for the older Banner, by the time his brothers touched their guns he was already dead, shot through the chest by the Gunsmith.

Clint Adams shot another brother through the chest before he could draw his gun, and by the time he turned to face the other two, they were already slumping to the floor, victims of the bartender's blazing Peacemakers.

Clint holstered his own gun and walked over to where the youngest of the Banner brothers lay. He used his boot to turn him over. In death the boy looked even younger than the nineteen he probably was.

"Damned shame," he said.

The bartender, having holstered his Colts, came up next to him and said, "You did what you could to avoid this."

"Not enough, obviously," Clint replied. He looked at the smaller man and said, "I'm much obliged to you for your help."

"I figured even the Gunsmith could use a hand," the man answered.

Clint turned to face the man fully and said, "Can I know the name of the man who saved my life?"

"I don't know if I saved your life," the man said, "but my name is Frank Leslie."

"Buckskin Frank Leslie?"

He saw the man wince, much the way he himself did whenever someone called him "The Gunsmith" to his face.

"I've been called that," Leslie admitted.

"I think I'd like to buy you a drink, Mr. Leslie," Clint said. "I believe we've got a lot in common."

"The name's Frank," Leslie said, "and since I own the place, the drink will be on me."

"Hadn't we better get your place cleaned up?" Clint asked as they walked to the bar.

Leslie turned and looked down at the four dead men, then said, "They're not going anyplace. We can tend to that after a drink, I think."

Clint looked at the bodies also, then shrugged and said to Leslie, "That's up to you, I guess. After all, it's your place."

"For at least two more days, it is," Leslie commented, and went around the bar for a bottle of whiskey.

"What's that mean?" Clint asked, leaning his elbows on the bar.

"Let's talk about that *after* we drink," Leslie said, setting a bottle of whiskey on the bar next to Clint's elbows. "This is the good stuff I'm breaking out, and I don't want to ruin the taste."

Chapter Three

Buckskin Frank Leslie had just finished explaining his situation to Clint when the local law arrived in the person of Sheriff Tom Sideman.

"All right, Leslie, what the hell happened here?" the lawman demanded. He was a tall, slender man in his late thirties who did not look like a lawman. He looked more like a newspaper editor, but in spite of appearances, he was a good and honest lawman, and he liked his town to be quiet and peaceful. He had been expecting that to change ever since Frank Leslie first arrived in town.

"Wasn't my fault, Sheriff—" Leslie began, but Clint interrupted him.

"It was my fault," he said.

"That's not true."

"Wait a minute," Sideman said, holding his hands up. "Just tell me what happened. Who are you, friend?"

"My name is Adams, Sheriff, Clint Adams."

The lawman obviously recognized the name and said, "That's just great. You're just what I needed. Is that your rig out front?"

"Yes, it is."

Sideman nodded, put his hands on his hips and said, "All right, tell me a story."

Clint and Frank Leslie exchanged glances, and it

was the Gunsmith who explained to the sheriff just what had occurred.

Sideman listened carefully, then looked at Frank Leslie who nodded his agreement with Clint's story.

"Who were the other customers, Leslie?" he finally asked, and Leslie mentioned one man's name, saying he didn't know who the other man was.

"All right, I'll check the story out with him, although I have to admit, I believe you."

"Thanks, Sheriff," Clint said.

"But that doesn't mean I'm happy," Sideman added. "Adams, are you planning on staying in town for any extended period of time?"

"I don't have definite plans yet, Sheriff, one way or the other."

"Well, let me know when you decide, will you?"

"Sure."

"I'll get some men to clean this place up."

"Much obliged, Sheriff," Leslie said, and the sheriff scowled and left.

"Why don't I go and find someplace to stay and then come back," Clint suggested. "We may have some things to discuss."

"Stay at the hotel down the street. It's the best one in town."

"Thanks," Clint said, pushing away from the bar, "and thanks again for the hand."

"Don't mention it. You would have done the same for me," Leslie said.

"Maybe," Clint said, "but you didn't know that when you stepped in, did you?"

Leslie just shrugged and poured himself another drink. He was thinking of how quickly promises you make to yourself fade away as Clint walked out and climbed onto his rig.

Chapter Four

With the team and Duke put up at the livery, Clint went to the hotel and got himself a room overlooking the street. He stowed his gear and went in search of a bath, which he found for two bits, with a shave thrown in for good measure. Policy of the hotel, he was told, for a new guest.

Something was on his mind the whole time, aside from the fact that he had killed two more men that day. (How many had he killed during his lifetime? he wondered. He was glad he didn't know, glad that he had never started to count—but, then, shouldn't a man know how many lives he had ended. . . .) He was thinking of Buckskin Frank Leslie, and his story. Clint knew who Frank Leslie was, as did many men who made their living with a gun. Leslie was fast, but had never become as well known as Hickok, or as the Gunsmith. Still, he had a reputation, and he was trying to lay it aside and settle down with a business. Clint admired that, just as he admired Leslie for stepping in when it looked like he was up against it—and Leslie had been right, Clint would have done the same thing in his place.

The business was what Clint was thinking most about, though. The Buckskin Saloon. According to Leslie, he was on the verge of losing the place because he couldn't make his payments, to a banker who made a habit of foreclosing on such mortgages.

Clad in clean, traildust-free clothes, Clint went to the front desk and asked the chicken-necked clerk where the telegraph office was. He followed the man's directions, found the office and sent a request off to Texas. When he got his reply, he went back to the Buckskin Saloon to discuss business with Frank Leslie.

"Back so soon?" Leslie asked. The place had filled up a bit more—with live, paying bodies.

"Looks like business is picking up," Clint remarked. "Regular customers, or bloodmongers, wanting to drink where four men died?"

"Regular customers," he said, then added, "although I'm sure a few of them are here to try and get a glimpse at the famous Gunsmith."

"Please," Clint said, wincing noticeably. "How about a drink?"

"Sure. Beer?"

"Fine."

When Leslie returned with the beer Clint said, "How is business, in general?"

"Well, you wouldn't know it to look at my books, but I could turn this place into something, given half the chance."

Clint turned to face the room with his beer in hand. It was not a large place, but it was big enough.

"Plans for any tables?" he asked.

"I'm not much of a gambler," Leslie admitted, "but I can see a few tables, some girls, and a lot of good whiskey and cold beer."

"Sounds about right," Clint said. "How much would you need to keep the wolves away from your door?"

Leslie thought it over a moment, then named a figure that he thought might do it.

"How would you feel about taking on a partner?" Clint asked, turning to face the bar again.

"A partner?"

Clint nodded and took a piece of paper out of his shirt pocket, which he handed to Leslie.

"What's this?" Buckskin Frank asked, then looked at it and raised his eyebrows.

"That's a draft drawn on my bank in Texas," Clint said. "It will enable you to make your back payments, with some left over to hold you for a few months until you can turn this place into a money-maker."

"Adams—"

"Clint," the Gunsmith corrected.

"Clint, you don't have to do this just because of what happened this morning," Leslie told him.

"Stop right there," Clint said. "Maybe that's part of the reason, but this money comes from an account I've had at that bank for years. There have been times when I've had nothing in my pocket but dust, and still never touched that account, but this place looks like a good investment to me, and if you don't mind, I'd like to buy in for a piece of the action."

Leslie's glance slid from Clint's face back to the numbers on the draft, and then he smiled and shook his head.

"This should hold us for a while, all right, but there's one thing I've got to warn you about before I accept it."

"What's that?"

"Sherman Jory."

"Who or what is that?"

"Jory is the bank manager, Clint, and he's had his eye on this place since I opened. He's not going to take kindly to your bailing me out."

"He'll get over it."

"He won't let go without some kind of a fight," Leslie warned further, "and he's got the men to fight with."

"A bank manager?"

"With ambitions."

"That's the worse kind," Clint said. He finished his beer and said, "How about another drink, to seal the deal?"

"The drink is to celebrate," Leslie said, "but a handshake seals the deal."

He stuck out his right hand, which Clint took, and the deal was sealed—along with their fate.

Chapter Five

Jesse Wells knocked on Sherman Jory's door and entered when he called out.

"Yes, Jesse?"

"Mr. Leslie is here to see you, Mr. Jory."

"Frank Leslie? Send him in."

Leslie squeezed past Jesse Wells, enjoying the close contact more than she did, and approached Jory's desk.

"That'll be all, Jesse. I'll call you if I need you," Jory said, dismissing his young secretary.

Jory looked the buckskin-clad man up and down with distaste and said, "What can I do for you?"

"Nothing," Leslie said. "I just came to give you something."

The banker tensed as Leslie moved his right hand, but the man ignored his gun and reached into his pocket. He came out with money and began counting it out. When he got to the exact amount he owed for two months, he dropped it on the desk and started for the door.

"Wait a minute—" Jory called out, standing up.

At the door Leslie turned and said, "Next month's payment will be on time, Jory. You can count on it."

"I'm glad to hear that."

"Sure you are."

"No, really, Leslie—but I am curious as to how you

18

came up with the money all of a sudden. Strike it rich?''

"I found a partner," Leslie told the banker. "Every man ought to have a partner, Jory. Somebody he can trust—but you wouldn't ever have to worry about that, would you, Jory? I mean, who would trust you?"

"A partner?" Jory asked, ignoring Leslie's remark. "Who did you find in this town to be your partner?"

"Not that it's any of your business, but nobody in this town is my partner. That is, nobody *from* this town," Leslie added. He opened the door and left before Jory could speak again.

A partner? Damn it, somebody had stepped in and ruined his plans, and he wanted to know who it was.

And he would know who it was, very soon!

Buckskin Frank Leslie left the bank feeling very pleased with himself, and with Clint Adams. Things were finally looking up and it took a man like the Gunsmith—a man with the same kind of past, who understood what he was trying to do—to bail him out. Now he only hoped that he would be able to use the time to turn the Buckskin Saloon into a real going concern.

When he reached the saloon Clint Adams was standing behind the bar, taking care of it until Leslie could return.

"You're back," Clint said as Leslie approached. They quickly changed places and Clint asked, "How did it go?"

"It was great," Leslie said, beaming. "You should have seen the look on old Sherman Jory's face when I laid that money down on his desk."

"I wish I could have," Clint said, "but somebody had to watch the store, right?"

"Right," Leslie agreed. He looked around at the customers standing at the bar, and seated at the tables, and said, "I can see I'm going to need some help here."

"You mean, hire somebody else to work the place?"

"Unless you have a better idea."

"As a matter of fact," Clint said, very thoughtfully, "I do."

"What? Not that you haven't already done enough."

"I'll stick around awhile," Clint said.

"You?"

"Sure. We can split the day between us and maybe, eventually, we can hire a girl—"

"A girl?"

"Sure, a pretty girl to circulate among the customers—"

"You don't mean a whore, do you?" Leslie asked. "I don't want to be running no whores—"

"No, no. Just a pretty girl, a barmaid," Clint broke in. "As soon as we can afford another salary."

"And how much time do you think you'll want to put into this here business?" Buckskin Frank asked.

"I don't rightly know, yet," Clint answered, "but you don't have to worry. For the most part I intend to be a silent partner—"

"Worry? I ain't worried, Clint," Leslie assured him. "Hell, I wouldn't mind if you wanted to be permanent."

"I don't know if it'll get that far," Clint said. "I don't know how long I can stay in one place."

"I know how you feel," Leslie said. "Sooner or later your past has to catch up with you."

"Right."

"Well, I've been here for eight months, and I intend to be here a lot longer," Buckskin Frank Leslie said. "I guess we could say that I was a test case. If it works for me, Clint, it can work for you."

"Well, I hope it works for you, Frank, I really do. I'll do anything I can to help."

"I appreciate that, Clint," Leslie said. "I hope it works for both of us. Why don't we get together after closing tonight and work out the details of our partnership?"

"That's fine with me. Want me to stick around now?"

"Why don't you go and get some dinner? Go out, make a right and walk down two blocks. The café there has pretty good food."

"Okay. I'll see you tonight."

"Partner," Buckskin Frank Leslie added, putting out his hand.

"Partner," the Gunsmith said, taking it.

Chapter Six

Clint followed Frank Leslie's directions and went to the café for dinner, but as soon as he walked in he saw something that made him think of things other than food.

The young lady was seated alone at a table in the center of the room. She had brown hair that was up in a bun, revealing a long, graceful, lovely neck. She was wearing wire-rim glasses, but behind the lenses her eyes were a soft, limpid brown. She was by no means stunning, but there was something about her that drew the eye. It was as if there was another woman inside of her, trying to get out and attract attention.

"Sir?" a waitress asked him. "Are you having dinner alone?"

"That remains to be seen," he replied. When the waitress frowned he smiled at her and said, "Can I have that table there?" pointing to the one nearest the brunette.

"Of course." She led him to the table and asked him if he would like to see a menu. "Do you have a specialty?" he asked. When she said that they did, he said the special would be fine, and ordered a pot of coffee to go with it.

From his new vantage point he could see that the woman at the next table was about twenty-two, and that beneath her demure dress her breasts were bold and firm. She seemed to sense that she was being watched and looked over at him. He smiled, and she squirmed slightly beneath his scrutiny and returned his smile. He took a deep breath, rose, and approached her table.

"Hello," he greeted her, smiling.

"Hello," she replied, returning his smile nervously. She seemed a bit skittish, like a young filly the first time a man tries to get near her. He wondered if this was indeed the first time, but decided no. She had a quality that would have been evident to other men. She had been approached before, certainly, but had she been touched?

"I'm sorry to disturb you, but I see that you haven't been served your dinner yet. Is that right?"

"Well, yes, that's right, but—"

"I'm a stranger in town—in fact, this is my first day here—and I really hate to eat alone. Would you mind if I joined you?"

"Well, I don't—"

"I would really appreciate it—I'll even pay for yours," Clint offered.

"Oh, that wouldn't be necessary," she assured him.

"Then you wouldn't mind sharing a table with me?" he asked, sitting down.

"Well . . ." she said, and then, as if she had just made the decision, added, "I don't see why not. It's the least I could do."

"Thank you, Miss—"

"Wells," she said, extending her hand across the table. "My name is Jesse Wells."

"Oh, like Jesse James."

"Yes," she said, smiling, and then with a frown, "I mean, no, not at all—I mean—"

"I was just making a joke," he assured her.

"Oh, I see," she said, although she didn't look too sure.

When the waitress came to the table with Jesse's food, Clint told her to bring his there, as well. The woman, a spinsterish-looking lady in her fifties, gave him a disapproving glance, but said, "Of course, sir."

"I really appreciate this," Clint said to Jesse Wells again.

"Oh, it's all right," she insisted. "I don't mind. You seem like a very nice man."

"Thanks. My name is Clint, by the way, Clint Adams. Listen, why don't you start to eat," he suggested. "I don't mind."

"Uh, thank you."

She had what looked like some kind of stew, with chunks of bread floating in it. It looked good.

"Is that the special?"

"Yes, it is. Did you order it?"

"Yes. Is it good?"

"Oh yes. I have it all the time."

"Then I'm glad I ordered it."

"You'll like it," she said.

Conversation got kind of slow following that exchange, and the waitress finally arrived with his order.

"Is everything all right, Miss Wells?" she asked the girl.

"Oh, everything is fine, Marge," Jesse Wells told the waitress, mistakenly thinking that the woman was asking about the food. "Just delicious, as always."

"Was there something wrong with your table, sir?" she asked Clint.

"No, the table was fine," he said. "I just didn't like the company."

"But there was no one sitting with you," Jesse said.

The waitress looked at the girl, then walked away shaking her head in wonderment.

Clint tasted the stew and found that it was indeed very good.

"Hey, you were right," he told Jesse. "It's delicious."

"I'm glad you like it."

"Have you lived in this town long?"

"All my life."

"What do you do?"

"I work at the bank," she said. "I'm a teller, and kind of the manager's helper."

"Sounds like a nice job."

"It's not bad, I suppose. What do you do, Clint?"

"I'm a gunsmith. I travel around with my wagon, selling and repairing guns."

"I'm afraid you won't find much business here in Brightwater," she said.

"Oh? Why is that?"

"This is a quiet town. There's never much need for a gun, here."

Clint guessed that she knew nothing about the shooting that had taken place earlier.

"You must have a good lawman here."

"Tom Sideman?" she said, looking as if she were about to laugh. "Tom's all right. He's a nice man, but he's more suited to what he used to do."

"Which was?"

"He used to be the schoolteacher."

Clint stared at her and said, "And now he's the sheriff? How did that happen?"

"Tom said he got tired of being a teacher and wanted a change."

"Some change, huh?"

"I suppose," she said. "He's a nice guy, but I think he's lucky that he's sheriff of Brightwater and not some other town."

"How did he get the job? Open election?"

"Election?" she said. "Nobody else wanted the job so he asked for it."

"Has he been good at it?"

"I have to give him credit," she admitted. "He's handled everything that's come along."

"Can't ask a man to do more than that," Clint commented.

She looked at him as if he had just said something very meaningful and said, "No, I guess you can't."

There was another lull in the conversation while they finished their dinner, and then Clint shared his coffee with her. He was trying to figure her out, and finally decided that she was simply a nice, not-too-bright girl who had never seen anything outside of Brightwater, Arizona, probably never would—and probably never wanted to.

He wondered how she would react if he offered her a job in the Buckskin Saloon.

No, he told himself. *Why ruin a budding friendship?*

"Well, I have to go," she said.

"Can I walk you home?"

"That's not necessary," she said, standing up.

"Let me pay for your dinner, then."

"No, please, I can do that. It was nice talking to you, Clint, and nice meeting you."

"I hope we get another opportunity to eat together," he said.

"That would be nice," she said, politely. She touched his arm and felt an odd sensation pulse through her as she told him, "You're a nice man, Clint Adams."

He smiled and said, ''You're a nice girl,'' and meant it literally.

Maybe too nice, he added to himself as he watched her walk from the restaurant. He shrugged, gave up the plans he'd been making, and called for his check.

Chapter Seven

Clint arrived at the Buckskin just as Frank Leslie was locking up.

"Good timing," Leslie said, stepping aside to allow the Gunsmith to enter. "What'd you do all evening."

"I had dinner with a very nice young lady and then found a poker game."

"How did you do?"

"I lost, and I won."

"In that order, eh?"

"In that order."

"Drink?" Leslie asked, heading for the bar.

"A beer."

"Who was the girl?"

"Jesse Wells, she said her name was," Clint answered, taking the glass of beer from his new friend and partner's hand.

"Wells?" Leslie asked, frowning.

"Yeah, why?"

"Name sounds familiar. What's she look like?"

Clint described her and halfway through his description Leslie brought his hand down on the top of the bar with a bang and said, "That's why the name sounded familiar. She works for Sherman Jory!"

"That's right," Clint said, remembering their conversation. "She did say she worked in the bank."

"She's not bad looking, either."

"No, she's just . . . too nice."

"She needs a man to bring her out, is all," Leslie said, leaning on the bar.

"You volunteering?"

"Not me. I like my women more experienced."

"There's no substitute for experience, all right," Clint agreed, "but there's also something to be said for educating a novice."

"Finish that beer," Leslie suggested, "and we'll take a bottle of whiskey over to a table and work out our terms."

Clint chugged the beer down and they retired to a table. Working out the terms of their partnership was the least of their conversation, and pretty soon—tongues loosened by liquor and good company—they began to talk about their pasts.

Clint told Leslie how he started out as a lawman in Oklahoma, after coming west when he was barely twenty. Educated in the East, he then began his new education, because living in the East and living in the West were as different as night and day. He took to his new education quickly, especially when it came to guns, and soon he was repairing and then constructing his own weapons, instituting modifications such as taking a Colt design and building a double-action, solid-body revolver that the world at large would not hear of for years.

Leslie said that he was born in Kentucky during the 1850's, and that his early education had included firearms—learning to use them that is, not to build them. He still left the building and repairing to others.

Clint had heard of Buckskin Frank Leslie, and that he was lightning fast with his twin Colts, with either hand. Had he a mind to, now with Wild Bill dead and the Gunsmith attempting to keep a low profile, he probably could have built his reputation up to their status. Obviously, however, Leslie did not have a mind to do that, and Clint respected him for it.

Leslie had heard much about the Gunsmith. Some people went so far as to say that Adams was even faster than Wild Bill Hickok, although no one would ever know now that the legendary Hickok was dead, killed by a coward's bullet in the back of the head. Leslie could not help but wonder how he would have stacked up against Bill, and now against the Gunsmith, Clint Adams.

"Do you ever shoot at targets?" he asked Clint.

"Never," Clint replied. "I never take my gun out unless it's to clean it, repair it . . . or use it. Bill was a great one for shooting targets, and sometimes he was even outshot."

"Was he ever outdrawn, though?"

"Not to my knowledge," Clint said, staring morbidly into his glass. The loss of Bill Hickok had affected him deeply and it had taken him some time to get to the point where he could talk freely about his friend.

"Bill could outdraw God and shoot the horns off the devil," he told Leslie, upending the bottle and pouring himself another drink.

"I've heard the same about you," Leslie said. "How did you stack up against Hickok?"

"We neither of us ever cared to find out," Clint replied. "Frankly, I still don't really care. Bill was my friend."

"I understand," Leslie said, filling his own glass. "I'm sorry I brought it up."

"If you're entertaining the thought of shooting targets with me, then I might as well mount up—"

"No, no," Leslie assured him. "I had no such thoughts." He raised his glass to Clint and said, "Here's to a new partnership."

"Good for as long as it lasts," Clint added, and they clinked glasses and drank.

Chapter Eight

Sherman Jory peered down at the head of the dark-haired girl who was working between his legs with her mouth, trying—as she had been for the past ten minutes—to get him hard. Her name was Lila, and she was from Kelly's House of Leisure. Right now, he and the girl were at his home, a large wood frame house at the north end of town, and it was late at night, which was the only time he had girls from Kelly's come to visit him. The town fathers knew that he owned property in Brightwater, but it wouldn't seem proper to them for the bank manager to own the local whorehouse.

As the girl continued to suck his limp cock, there was a knock at the door.

"In the bedroom," he told the girl. She got up from her knees and padded naked into the bedroom without a word. She was young, about nineteen, and she was the newest girl at Kelly's. She knew she was auditioning for her job at Kelly's and couldn't understand why she'd been having so much trouble getting Jory hard—unless he was just too old.

Jory pulled on his silk robe and went to answer the door. As he had expected, it was Martin Cort.

"You wanted me?" Cort asked as he entered.

"Where have you been?" Jory demanded. "I've had people looking for you for hours."

"I was busy."

As Cort turned to face Jory following his remark, Jory slapped him across the right side of the face. It wasn't much of a slap and Cort's head barely moved, but his face flushed red as a result, more from anger and frustration. As for Jory, as a result of the slap, he finally felt himself getting hard.

Cort stared at Jory with his fists clenched at his sides.

''That is not the kind of answer I expect from my employees, Cort'' Jory told him, tightly. ''Where the hell have you been?''

''I was getting laid,'' Cort replied.

''You were not at Kelly's,'' Jory told him. ''I checked.''

''I was with Lucie Ellis.''

Jory's jaw dropped and he said, ''The mayor's daughter? Are you crazy?''

''I visit her every once in a while,'' Cort said, unclenching his fists. He knew that Jory and Mayor Ellis were friends, and he was enjoying Jory's reaction to his statement.

''The girl is only eighteen,'' Jory said.

''She sure fucks older,'' Cort replied.

''That's enough!'' Jory snapped. ''I don't want to hear any more.''

He walked past Cort to a small portable bar and poured himself a brandy without offering Cort any. It wasn't the fact that Cort had been with the daughter of his friend that had upset him, but the fact that the man had done what he had been wanting to do since the first time he noticed how the girl had been growing up. A year ago he noticed how she had blossomed into a lovely young woman, and he'd been having fantasies about her ever since. Dinner at the Ellis house had come to be a painful experience as he found himself invariably seated across from the girl, struggling with a raging erection. And what's more, the little bitch knew it.

He drank half the brandy, then turned to Cort, having composed himself sufficiently to talk to the man.

"All right, never mind that," he said.

"What did you want to see me about?"

"Frank Leslie came into the bank today and paid what he owed on his note."

"What? Where did he get the money?"

"He said that he now has a partner."

"Somebody we know?"

"No, apparently an out-of-towner. I want you to find out who the man is."

"And?"

"Just find out and let me know. I'll tell you if and when I want you to do something about it."

Cort did not look happy as he absently laid his hand on the butt of his gun.

"Don't get trigger-happy, god damn it!" Jory snapped as he noticed. "You do what you're told, Cort, and that's all!" he told the gunman, pointing with his index finger.

"Yes, sir," Cort replied. At that moment he didn't know who he was more angry with, himself or Jory. The time would come, he thought . . .

"That's all. Get out," Jory commanded curtly, pouring himself another drink.

Cort looked over at the closed bedroom door and suddenly knew that Jory had one of the girls from Kelly's in there waiting for him. *I hope you can't get it up, you old bastard*, he said to himself.

"Good night," he said aloud to Jory, and left, closing the door behind him.

Jory finished his second brandy, enjoying the feeling of power that always came over him when he dealt with Cort. The man was a gunman and was physically capable of killing him with his bare hands, yet it was Jory who was in control. That and thoughts of Lucie Ellis had given him a wild, pulsating erection. He put down his empty glass and walked to the bedroom door, slamming it open. On the bed the girl started at his violent entrance. She got up and stood there, naked, staring at him. She was not particularly pretty, but she had a good body. Her breasts were small, but firm, her belly was flat, but suddenly, the thing that excited him most was her hair. It was about the same color and length as Lucie Ellis's hair.

He loosened the belt on his robe, and opened it. He hadn't been this hard and long for years. Her eyes widened and he enjoyed the look on her face as she inspected him.

"Oh, Mr. Jory," she gasped.

He dropped his robe to the floor so that he was totally naked.

He moved forward until he was directly in front of her and she put her hands on his barrel chest, wrapping her fingers in the mass of gray hair she found there. She let her hands slide down his body until she was holding his hard dick in her hands.

"Turn around and bend over," he commanded, suddenly.

"Don't you want me to—" she started to ask, but he slapped her across the face and repeated, "Turn around."

Rubbing her cheek she whispered, "Yes, Mr. Jory," and did as he said.

She leaned on the bed and hiked her ass in the air for him. He moved forward, took her hips in his hands and drove himself into her cunt from behind with tremendous force.

"Ooh!" she squealed, pushing back against him.

From this angle he would be able to take her and pretend that she was Lucie Ellis.

Chapter Nine

A few weeks passed during which Clint had set up a house poker game, with himself as the dealer. This brought in enough extra customers to enable Leslie and Clint to hire a girl who had quit Kelly's to work the place. It was amazing how many cowhands and drifters were eager to lose their money in a house game—and for the first time in his life, Clint found the poker odds in his favor.

The girl called herself Joy Darling, and it was her experience that got her the job. When asked if she was expected to work ''hard''—which meant was she expected to sleep with customers—Clint told her that would be up to her. If she chose to do so, any money she made would be hers.

Joy was a tall, slim blonde, which made her round, heavy breasts look even heavier and during the two weeks she had been working at the saloon, she had not had sex with any of the customers, for money or otherwise. In fact, the only person she had been having sex with was the Gunsmith—for free.

Clint was holding those large breasts together now, sucking on both nipples at once while she sat astride him, riding his rigid penis. It was obvious that she enjoyed sex more than almost any other woman he had ever met, so he wondered why she was not selling it to the customers.

''Ooh, God,'' she cried out as she felt his penis swell

and then begin to spurt furiously, "it feels like I'm on fire!"

He abandoned her breasts and cupped her buttocks as she began to bounce uncontrollably on top of him, to keep his cock from slipping free before he was finished.

"God, I'm coming!" she cried. She fell flat on top of him, crushing those marvelous breasts against his chest, and fused her mouth to his, her tongue lashing out at his wildly.

When they were finished he decided to go ahead and ask her the question.

"I've been waiting for you to ask me that," she said, lying beside him, toying with his penis. "It's not as if I haven't sold it before, because you know I have. I have no qualms about it, and I do enjoy sex—"

"I'll say," he interjected, and she gave him a playful squeeze.

"The simple fact of the matter is that I enjoy it when it's free, when I'm doing it because I want to, and not because I'm being paid to. When there's money involved, then I'm working."

"I suppose that makes sense, but we're not paying you all that much, Joy."

"I know, but it's enough, and the work is easy," she explained. "I've worked 'hard' before," she went on, "and I probably will again . . . but not for a while."

"Now another question," he said, sitting up.

"Oh, no," she shouted, jumping out of bed before he could. "You're not going to ask me my real name again, and you're not going to beat me to the bath this morning."

With that she ran from the room naked, down the hall and into the bathroom. A few seconds later, Leslie came walking into the room.

"That girl sure bounces when she runs, doesn't she?"

"She does that," Clint agreed. He got up from the bed and walked to the pitcher and bowl next to the window overlooking the street. They were on the second floor above the saloon, where Leslie, and now Clint, maintained a room. They did not have a room for Joy, so she lived in a roominghouse a couple of streets away—when she wasn't sleeping in Clint's bed.

Clint poured some water from the pitcher to the bowl then scooped it in his hands and washed his face and chest. Since Joy had gotten to the bath first, this would have to do. That woman spent almost as much time in the water as she did in bed.

"You know, we've got another payment to make to Sherman Jory," Leslie told Clint.

"How soon?" Clint asked through a towel.

"Four days."

"We've got the money, don't we?"

"And more, thanks to you. That poker game you set up really bailed us out . . . and the men who don't come to play come to look down Joy's bodice."

"I know," Clint said. "That girl could make herself a lot of money on the side if she'd a mind to."

"Guess she just doesn't have a mind to," Leslie replied. "Who's going to make the payment to Jory?"

"The note's in your name, isn't it?" Clint asked.

"Yep, but Jory's been wanting to meet my partner for so long I thought I'd let you take it over."

"Look, why don't you go downstairs and let me shave, and we'll talk about it later. Must be pretty close to noon, by now."

"Just about," Leslie verified. "Okay, I'll see you downstairs."

Clint finished shaving and dressing, and was buckling on his gun when Joy appeared again, wearing a robe tightly belted around her waist. She was still wet, and the robe molded itself to her curves like a second skin. Clint examined her critically, and although he loved her breasts and she was marvelous in bed, he sometimes wished she were more filled out in other areas.

"I know," she said squirming beneath his eyes. "I'm too skinny."

"I never said that."

"You don't have to. Actually, it's not that I'm skinny, it's just that my tits are too big."

He walked up to her, cupped her breasts and said, "I guess that's one way of looking at it."

He kissed her, and she opened her mouth wide and sucked his tongue in so she could chew on it a bit. He felt himself getting hard, and pushed her away gently, saying, "I've got to get downstairs."

She plastered herself against him and he could feel her nipples right through her robe and his shirt.

"I ain't going to make it easy for you to leave," she promised.

He slapped her on the behind and said, "Behave, woman."

He picked up his hat and headed for the door, but she called to him and asked, "Tonight?"

As many times as she had slept with Clint, she never took it for granted that it would happen again. He seemed to be working hard to keep her at arm's length. Afterward, she always asked the same question, and he always gave her the same answer.

"We'll see."

Chapter Ten

Lila Shore had become Sherman Jory's favorite whore because he could pretend that she was Lucie Ellis. She was waiting for him in his bedroom while he spoke to Martin Cort in his living room the night before Frank Leslie's next payment was due.

"From what I can make out," Martin Cort was saying, "they won't have any trouble making the next payment."

"Damn it!" Jory snapped, slamming his fist down on a nearby table.

"What do you want to do, Mr. Jory?"

Jory tugged at his beard as his mind raced.

"Let's wait until they make the payment tomorrow," he finally said, "and then we'll talk about what I want to do. Now get out."

Cort didn't mind following Sherman Jory's "suggestion" that he get out. He had a naked and willing Lucie Ellis waiting for him in a cabin he kept just outside of town.

"Good night," he said, and hurried out.

Jory slammed his fist down on the table again, then poured himself a short brandy and downed it. As he turned and stalked towards the bedroom door he was angry, and so was his rigid penis. Angry, red and pulsating. When he slammed the door open, Lila Shore looked up from the bed and knew what she was in for.

This was the damnedest man, she thought. He only liked to do it one way—

"Face down!" Jory ordered.

"Yes, Mr. Jory," Lila said obediently, slipping off the bed and assuming the position whereby she ceased to be Lila Shore and suddenly became Lucie Ellis.

The real Lucie Ellis, however, was lying on her back with her legs wrapped around Martin Cort's waist. As he plowed into her and she gasped and cried into his ears, Cort realized that if Frank Leslie and his partner, Clint Adams, made that payment tomorrow, Sherman Jory was not going to be in a very good mood. That meant that he might very well get the chance to finally face down and kill Buckskin Frank Leslie . . . with the famous Gunsmith thrown in for good measure.

A man never felt so powerful and fearless as when he was between a woman's legs.

Chapter Eleven

The following morning Clint Adams walked into the bank and spotted Jesse Wells. She looked pert and pretty, and he approached her desk.

"Good morning, Miss Wells."

She looked up at him, frowned, adjusted her glasses on her cute nose, and then recognized him.

"Mr. Adams."

"Clint."

"How are you?"

"I'm just fine," he said. "You are looking extremely well. Very pretty, in fact."

She adjusted her glasses self-consciously and said, "How kind of you. Is there something I can help you with?"

"I'd like to see Mr. Jory."

"Do you have an appointment?"

"No, but I'm sure he'll be expecting me," he said, then added, "either myself or Frank Leslie, that is."

"Do you know Mr. Leslie?"

"We're partners," Clint replied. "I have this month's payment on his note."

"You are his partner in the Buckskin Saloon?" she asked, frowning.

"That's right."

"I understood you were a stranger in town when we met, Mr. Adams."

"I was, Miss Wells, and I'm surprised we haven't run into each other since then."

Actually, it was no surprise. Clint had taken to having most of his meals brought in to the saloon.

"I'll tell Mr. Jory that you're here."

"Much obliged, Miss Wells."

He watched as she walked to a door at the rear of the room, knocked and entered. A few moments later she came out, closing the door behind her, and came back to her desk.

"You can go right in, Mr. Adams," she informed him.

He walked to the door, knocked and entered. The man behind the desk was white-haired, full-bearded and barrel-chested. He stood and said, "Welcome, Mr. Adams. I understand that you have something for me."

"Indeed I do, Mr. Jory," Clint said. He took an envelope from his pocket and dropped it on Jory's desk. It contained the exact amount due on Frank Leslie's note for that month.

"This month's payment?" Jory asked, and Clint nodded. The bank man stared down at the envelope, then said, "Why don't you have a seat, Mr. Adams? Let's have a chat, shall we?"

"What have we to chat about?" Clint asked, still standing.

"I'm curious about why a stranger in Brightwater would suddenly become partners with a man in a losing endeavor."

"Losing?" Clint asked. "Who said the saloon was losing?"

"Isn't it?"

"One of us will be in each month with our payment,

Mr. Jory, until the note is paid off. You can count on that.''

''I see. Well, for your sake I hope you're right, Mr. Adams,'' Jory said, picking up the envelope with that month's payment.

''I'll bet you do,'' Clint said. ''Good day, Mr. Jory.''

''Good day, Mr. Adams.''

Clint turned and left Jory's office, stopping by Jesse Wells's desk before leaving the bank.

''I hope to see you again soon, Miss Wells,'' he said. ''Outside of this bank, that is.''

Before she had a chance to reply, he left and went back to the saloon.

''Make the payment?'' Leslie asked.

''I made it. Mr. Jory was very gracious and wished us luck making future payments.''

''I'll bet he did.''

''It seems Mr. Jory is under the impression that this is a losing proposition.''

''Is that a fact? Won't he be surprised when we continue to meet our payments?''

''I hope he is,'' Clint said. ''How about a beer, partner?''

''Coming right up, partner.''

At that moment, however, Sherman Jory was making plans to take steps to see to it that the owners of the Buckskin Saloon were not able to make any more payments.

And wouldn't they be surprised when that happened?

Chapter Twelve

Elroy James was one of the Jamison Liquor Company's western representatives, and the wagonload of liquor he was now transporting to Brightwater, Arizona was earmarked for the Buckskin Saloon. Five cases in all, a large supply for a saloon that had barely enough money for one case the month before. Business must be booming in Brightwater, James thought.

He was ten miles north of Brightwater when the three men on horseback appeared—with their guns out.

"Pull up," one of them ordered. They were all wearing bandanas over the lower portion of their faces, but this man appeared to be the leader.

"Mister, did you pick the wrong wagon to rob," Elroy James told the man. "All I got back there is whiskey, and all I got in my pockets is—"

"Whiskey's what we want," the man said, cutting him off. "All right, boys," he said to the other two, and they cocked the hammers back on their pistols and opened fire on the cases of whiskey. By the time they stopped firing, each case had sprung several leaks, and whiskey was soaking through the bed of the wagon to the ground below.

"Jesus Christ," James yelled, "what in tarnation did you do that for? I'll bet there ain't a bottle left in one piece back there."

''That was the idea, friend,'' the leader said, holstering his gun.

''Do you know how long it'll take to replace that whiskey?'' James demanded. ''You know how long my customer is gonna have to wait now?''

''Yep,'' the masked leader said, ''that was the idea, too. Why don't you continue on your way now, friend, while you're still in one piece.''

''Me?'' James replied. Suddenly he realized that he was in danger of springing as many leaks as those liquor cases in the wagon.

''I'm going,'' he said hastily, ''I'm going.''

''Go on,'' the man said. ''Deliver your whiskey to your customer, with our compliments.''

Chapter Thirteen

Some time later Frank Leslie came out of the back storeroom carrying two jagged bottle necks that were still dripping whiskey and showed them to Clint, who was behind the bar.

"What the hell is that?" Clint asked.

"This," Leslie said, putting the pieces on the bar-top, "is our new shipment of whiskey."

"What did you do, drop a case?"

"Somebody shot up the shipment, Clint," Leslie said. "Three men stopped the shipment, shot it up and then told our rep, Elroy James, to go ahead and make the delivery."

They both leaned on the bar and stared down at the jagged chunks of glass, and then Clint looked at Leslie and said, "Jory."

"Who else?" his partner replied, then added, "And I'll bet it was Martin Cort who did the dirty work."

"Any of it get through in one piece?"

"Half a dozen bottles, maybe," Leslie said. "We might be able to drain out a few more bottles, if we want to take a chance on somebody swallowing some glass."

"Bad for business," Clint said, shaking his head.

"We can't last more than a day, Clint," Leslie said. "We're going to run out of whiskey."

"How are we on beer?"

"We got plenty of beer, and some belly-burning rotgut, but the good stuff ain't going to last a day."

"We've got to get more whiskey," Clint said, unnecessarily.

"But where?"

"Is our man still here?"

"Yeah, but he says he can't replace the shipment for at least a week, maybe ten days, and even if he does we'll have to pay for both."

"He delivered it damaged," Clint pointed out.

"You want to fight him on it and wait even longer for a replacement shipment?"

"All right, so we'll pay for both, but we've got to do something in the meantime." Clint prodded the broken bottle ends with his finger and said, "We'll think of something."

"Well, let me know when we do."

As Leslie started to walk away Clint grabbed his arm and said, "Wait a minute."

"What? Did we think of something already?"

"No, but wait here and let me talk to this Elroy James."

"Go ahead. Maybe you'll have better luck than I did."

Clint went into the storeroom, found it empty, then went out back where Elroy James was trying to dry off the bed of his wagon.

"Just because I deliver liquor in it don't mean it's got to smell like it," he was saying to himself.

"Mr. James?" Clint called.

"Yeah," the man called back, looking up. "You Mr. Leslie's new partner?"

"That's right."

James came off the wagon with his hand outstretched, saying, "Glad to meet you."

"Likewise," Clint said, taking the man's hand.

James was a small man, with a lot of nervous energy, and he spoke in quick, clipped words and sentences.

"Understand you've kind of turned this business around."

"I helped," Clint said. "Listen, about this incident—"

"Hey, I don't make the rules," James said quickly, holding up his hands. "You got to pay for this shipment—"

"I'm not arguing that," Clint said, cutting the man off.

"You're not?"

"No we'll pay for this shipment. That's not the problem. The problem is getting more whiskey fast."

"Getting more whiskey is no problem," James said, then added, "but fast . . . that's a problem."

"Well, let's do something about it," Clint suggested.

"I would like to help you—"

"Make a suggestion," Clint said, putting his hand in his pocket.

"I'd really like to take your money," James said, "but it wouldn't help."

"It wouldn't?"

James shook his head. "I'll do the best I can, Clint, I promise. I like to keep my customers happy."

"That's very—how many customers do you have in this area?"

"Just two," James said. "You and Kelly's."

"And you've got a shipment for them?"

"Right."

"When are you delivering their whiskey?"

"Tomorrow. Soon as I get back I'll load up and bring it on over. After that, I'll try and push through a second shipment for you."

"That's fine, Mr. James."

"Elroy."

"I appreciate all of your help, Elroy."

"I like to keep my customers happy," James said, putting his hand out.

Clint took it and said, "That's admirable."

"Well, I got to get going," James said. "I'm really sorry about this, but there wasn't much that I could do. Not looking at three guns."

"I understand," Clint assured him. "You weren't able to see any of their faces at all?"

"Nope," James said, climbing aboard his wagon. "And their voices—well, the leader's was muffled by the bandana."

"The others didn't speak?"

"Nope, they just did the shooting. The leader did the talking."

"I see."

"I got to be on my way."

"Sure, go ahead," Clint said, then under his voice he added, "I think I've got all I need."

Chapter Fourteen

"That's illegal," Buckskin Frank Leslie said.

"We'll pay them back. Besides, I'm sure they've got plenty to tide them over. That's an impressive operation they've got going."

"I thought you didn't pay for your, uh, 'leisure.' "

"I don't. I've walked past, and it's an impressive looking operation. Look, they'll never miss the stuff."

"Are you sure you used to be a lawman?

The fact of the matter was that for the first time in a long time, Clint Adams was having fun.

Clint pulled the bandana up over the lower portion of his face, then rode out into the road to stop Elroy James. There was one thing he wouldn't do as part of the charade, and that was remove his gun from his holster. If James resisted at all, he'd give it up rather than pull his gun.

But James didn't resist. As soon as he saw the masked man in his path, he pulled up and put his hands in the air. Whiskey just wasn't worth dying for, and although the man did not have his gun out, James felt sure he would be able to produce it in a hurry.

"Go ahead," he said, resignedly. "Shoot it up."

"I don't want to shoot it up," Clint said from behind the bandana.

"You don't?"

"Just get down, take off a half dozen cases and put them on the side of the road."

"Then what?"

"Then you can be on your way."

James frowned, wondering if he were being told the truth. A more imaginative man might have figured it all out, but James just jumped down, unloaded six cases of whiskey meant for Kelly's, and then waited for further instructions.

"Okay, that's it," Clint told him. "Climb aboard and move on."

"You mean I can go?"

"You can go."

Clint moved Duke out of the way, and James climbed aboard and lit out for town. Clint waited until James's wagon had faded from sight, then pulled the bandana down and yelled out, "All right, bring it out!"

From behind a clump of trees Frank Leslie drove a buckboard, bringing it over to where Elroy James had unloaded six cases of whiskey.

Climbing down he asked Clint, "Why six?"

"One for good luck," Clint said, dismounting to help load the cases. "Besides, asking for five would have been too much of a coincidence."

"I think he was too scared to notice."

"Maybe so," Clint said. "Come on, let's get this stuff loaded."

"You're enjoying this, aren't you?" Leslie asked Clint, almost accusingly.

"Just trying to keep our business going, partner," Clint explained. "Like I said, we'll pay it all back."

As they bent over to pick up a carton, Leslie said again, "Are you sure you used to be a lawman?"

"Just load."

Sherman Jory slammed his fist down on his desk top and bellowed, "My own whiskey, damn it!"

"How can we be sure it was them?" Cort asked.

Jory waved the question away with an angry sweep of his arm. "Who else could it be?"

"Why didn't they take the whole shipment?"

"How many cases did you and the boys shoot up?"

"I didn't count," Cort said, "but it couldn't have been more than five or six."

"And they took six. I don't believe in coincidence, Cort."

Martin Cort was actually enjoying Jory's reaction to this latest turn of events. Katie Kelly, the middle-aged madam who ran Kelly's for Jory, reported the incident to Cort, who had immediately gone to the bank to inform his employer.

"The gall!" Jory snapped angrily. "It had to be this Adams's idea. I don't think Leslie has that much imagination."

"Adams is a sharp one, all right," Cort said.

Jory gave his man a long look and then said, "You sound as if you know him."

It was Cort's turn to give his employer a disbelieving look as he asked, "Don't you know who Clint Adams is?"

"Should I?"

"I'll be damned," Cort said, looking at the ceiling. "It never occurred to me that you wouldn't."

"Well, who is he, damn it! Some kind of gunman? What do I know about gunmen? I'm a businessman!"

"He's the Gunsmith, man," Cort said. "Don't you

know who the Gunsmith is?''

Jory hesitated, because the name did ring some kind of a bell with him.

"As I said, some kind of gunman," he replied.

"With a big rep," Cort added, "bigger even than Buckskin Frank Leslie."

"Indeed?"

"Yeah, but I can take them both," Cort bragged, but it was a brag that his employer ignored.

"The Gunsmith, eh? And Buckskin Frank Leslie. Two of a kind. Very interesting."

The whiskey exchange was all but forgotten now, as a new plan began to formulate in Sherman Jory's mind.

Chapter Fifteen

"It's been too quiet this past week," Clint said to Joy Darling as they lay in Clint's bed together.

"What do you mean?"

"I don't think Jory would try that trick with the whiskey and then not react when we retaliated."

"Are you sure it's Mr. Jory?" she asked.

"Why?"

"Well, most folks in this town think he's a perfect gentleman."

"I know," Clint said. And he did, from the bar talk he'd been involved in. Didn't anyone else know what the man was really like? Oh, they knew he owned a few businesses in town, but he must have gone after some of them the way he was going after the Buckskin Saloon. You'd think someone would know him for what he was.

"He's got the whole town on a string, I think," Clint said. "Maybe we should let them know what he's really about."

"You're gonna tell them?"

"I don't know that they'd believe me," Clint said, "but maybe we can show them. They'd have to believe their own eyes, wouldn't they?" he asked.

"Most people would," she agreed. "Do you need any help?"

His first thought was to say no, but he changed his mind and said, "Maybe you could just keep your ears open, see what you can find out from some of the people."

"The women, you mean?"

"Yes," he said, "and not just the ones you meet in the dress shop."

"The working girls, you mean?"

"Maybe they'll know something the supposedly decent women don't know."

Joy batted her eyelids at Clint innocently and said, "That's a bit of an understatement, don't you think?"

Chapter Sixteen

"We've got an invitation," Frank Leslie told Clint when he came down that morning.

"To what?"

"A barbecue at Wesley Ellis's ranch."

"The mayor?"

"The same—and a very good friend of banker Jory."

"What's the occasion?"

"It's sort of a businessman's barbecue, from what I understand. They have it every year. All of the merchants are invited out there for a feast. I think it's supposed to bring the townspeople closer together."

"Just what we need," Clint said, "to rub elbows with Sherman Jory."

"Shall we go?"

"I don't think we should miss it. We can get someone to watch the store, can't we?"

"I'm sure of it. Besides, Joy will be here."

"When is this wingding?"

"Tomorrow afternoon."

"What wingding?" Joy asked from behind.

Damn the woman, Clint thought, *she picks the wrong time to come down early. She isn't going to like being left behind.*

"Just a little business meeting out at the mayor's ranch tomorrow," Clint said to her.

"Oh, you mean the barbecue?"

"You know about that?"

"Hey, you forget. This time last year I was working at Kelly's. I know all about the barbecue. Are you both planning on going?"

"We were, yeah."

"Okay, well, I can take care of the place while you're gone. There won't be that much morning and afternoon business."

"Maybe you should open at twelve instead of eleven," Leslie suggested.

"Whatever you guys want," she said. "It's your place." She looked directly at Clint and asked, "You didn't think I was going to make a fuss about tomorrow, did you?"

"Me? Why would I?" he asked innocently.

"Just thought I'd ask. I'm very understanding, you know."

"I'm well aware of that," he said.

She was wearing one of her simple dresses instead of her spangled work dress. "I'm going to do some shopping," she said. "I'll see you both later."

"Okay," Clint said.

After she had gone Leslie said to Clint, "You're closer to her than I am—"

"Slightly."

"What I mean is, why do you think she quit working at Kelly's to work here?"

"She didn't quit Kelly's to work here," Clint pointed out. "She quit Kelly's, and then we hired her."

"It amounts to the same thing."

"I guess she just got tired of having to have sex with strangers," Clint said.

"For a lot of money," Leslie added.

"It's possible, Frank."

"Well, let's see how long she lasts on what we're paying her."

"She'll probably outlast me," Clint said, pushing away from the bar.

"You getting the itch to move?" Leslie asked.

"Not yet," Clint answered, "but I am going to go out and give Duke some exercise before we open."

"Wish you'd let me do that. That's just about the best looking animal I've ever seen."

"Just about?" Clint asked.

Chapter Seventeen

Clint admitted to himself that he had been neglecting Duke ever since getting involved with Frank Leslie and the Buckskin Saloon. The only extended ride he'd had on the big black was when he rode out to "borrow" the whiskey from Elroy James.

"Come on, big fella," he told Duke, leading him out of the livery stable. "We're going to take a nice long ride."

He mounted up and started riding down Brightwater's main street. As he approached the stagecoach stop he saw the banker, Sherman Jory, standing there, looking at his pocket watch, and he couldn't resist stopping.

"Good morning, Mr. Jory," he said, reining Duke in right in front of the white-haired banker.

Jory looked up, squinted against the glare of the sun and recognized Clint.

"Mr. Adams," he said in a neutral tone. "Good morning, sir. Out for a morning ride?"

"Just giving my horse some exercise."

"That's a magnificent looking animal," Jory said, sounding sincere for a change.

"Thank you. Are you waiting for the stage?"

"Yes, I'm, er—" the man started to answer, but then he seemed to think better of it. "Yes, I'm waiting for someone."

"You seem pretty anxious."

"I—uh—just have a lot of work waiting for me back at the bank," Jory said.

"Oh? A rash of foreclosures?"

Jory was about to reply when the stage pulled onto the street and approached the stop. Clint walked Duke away from the stop and then simply waited and watched. He was curious to see who Jory was waiting for, and why he was so nervous about it.

Several male passengers disembarked from the stage before a young lady appeared and Jory rushed to help her step down.

"Daddy," Clint heard the girl say, and he sat up straighter in an attempt to get a good look at her. She appeared to be about nineteen, with long red hair and a figure that was almost plump, but pleasingly so.

Jory threw a glance over at Clint—a somewhat apprehensive glance, at that—and then threw one arm around the girl's shoulder and attempted to hurry her away.

"Oh, my bags," the girl said. She executed a very graceful turn away from her father, evading his arm, and in doing so her eyes met Clint's head on. Her face was an incredible combination of sweetness and sensuality. Her eyes were wide and innocent, while her mouth was wide with an especially heavy underlip.

"Your bags will be taken care of, dear," her father said, trying to hurry her away again.

"Oh, what a beautiful animal," the girl cooed, and Clint assumed she was talking about Duke. "May we take a closer look?"

"Dear, I really do have a lot of work—" her father protested, but she turned the full power of her eyes on him and said, "Oh, may we, please? For a moment?"

Her father melted and said, "As you wish."

They walked down the boardwalk together, and although the girl had professed to want a closer look at Duke, her eyes were in fact on Clint.

"You have a beautiful horse, sir," she said to him, reaching a hand out to touch Duke's nose.

"Be careful of his teeth, miss," Clint warned. "Sometimes he bites."

"Oh, you wouldn't bite me, would you, you beautiful boy?" she asked Duke, gently stroking his nose.

"You have a way with horses, I see," Clint said.

"Dear, we must go," her father insisted.

"I had no idea that you had such a lovely daughter, Mr. Jory," Clint said.

"Oh," the girl said, "do you know each other?"

"Your father and I have done some business together."

"Really?" She turned to her father and said, "You should introduce us, Father."

"Your father has a lot of work at the bank, Miss Jory," Clint said. "My name is Clint Adams."

"I am Marlene Jory, Mr. Adams, and I've just returned from attending school in the East." Her eyes locked onto his boldly and she said, "I've learned a great many things back East."

"I'm sure you have, miss."

"Since you've done business with my father, I assume you own a business in town."

"Yes, ma'am. The Buckskin Saloon."

"Then we'll see you at the mayor's barbecue tomorrow," she said, looking pleased.

"My partner and I will certainly be there."

"Oh, then I'm so glad I made it back in time to attend."

"Marlene, dear . . . " her father said, and Clint thought he could hear the bank man's teeth grinding.

"So nice to have met you, Mr. Adams," she said, giving Duke's nose a last rub. "I look forward to seeing you tomorrow."

"Until tomorrow, then," Clint said, and she allowed her father to finally pull her away.

Now Clint understood why Sherman Jory had been so nervous. The last thing the banker would have wanted was for Clint or Frank Leslie to find out that he had a daughter, let alone meet her.

That would just give them added ammunition, and now that Clint knew about the lovely and delectable Marlene Jory, he intended to fit her into his plans.

"Jory has a what?" asked Buckskin Frank Leslie.

"A daughter," Clint repeated. "And what a daughter."

"Where's he been hiding her?"

"Back East in school, somewhere, but she's here now, and Jory is very nervous about it."

"I can see how he would be," Leslie said. "I'm sure he wouldn't want either of us to know about her, let alone meet her."

"And now we've done both. You'll meet her tomorrow; she'll be at the barbecue with him."

"Do you think he'll allow her to come?"

"Having met and seen that young lady, Frank," Clint said sincerely, "I doubt that any man—even her father—could refuse her anything."

Chapter Eighteen

The mayor's ranch was such an impressive looking operation that Clint started to wonder if Mayor Wesley Ellis was more than just friends with Sherman Jory. Maybe Jory's association with the mayor was what gave him that veneer of respectability, but it might just as well work the other way, too.

"Partners," Clint said aloud as he and Frank Leslie rode up to the front of the main house.

"What?"

"Just thinking out loud."

While they were dismounting Clint said, "Don't the townspeople wonder how come the mayor can afford an outfit like this?"

"We're new here, Clint," Leslie reminded him. "There may be some things we're not aware of."

"Like what?"

"Like maybe he was a rancher before he became mayor."

Clint conceded that point to his partner, and they turned their horses over to a ranch hand, who promised to take proper care of Duke.

"Through the house or around it, but the barbecue's in the back," he told them before walking off with their animals.

They started to mount the steps to the front door

when Clint suddenly decided that it would be better if they went around.

"Why?" Leslie asked.

"Just humor me, okay?" Clint said. "I've just got a bad feeling."

"What's got into you?" Buckskin Frank asked his partner as they walked around the house.

"I just think we should keep in mind the fact that Mayor Ellis and Sherman Jory are very close."

"You think they might try something?"

"It's been a while since the business with the whiskey, Frank. I think he's overdue, don't you?"

When they got around to the back they found the barbecue in full swing. They milled about for a while, then found themselves standing off to one side together.

"Know anybody?" Clint asked.

"I can spot a customer or two, but I wouldn't say we had any real friends here."

"I'm starting to feel uncomfortable," Clint said, and as he said it he saw Sherman Jory with his daughter, Marlene, on his arm. On the other side of Marlene Jory, however, he saw a younger girl who put the older girl to shame.

"Who is that?" Clint asked.

"Is that Jory's daughter?"

"Yes, but who is that with her?"

"Oh, that's Mayor Ellis's daughter, Lucie. Amazing, isn't she?"

There was something about that girl that seemed to reach out and grab a man by the . . . throat, among other places. She was smaller than Marlene Jory, and much slimmer. She had small, pointed breasts, a tiny waist, and a face that was both gamin and sexy.

"They make quite a pair," Clint said. "How old is she?"

"Eighteen, I guess. Can't be much older than that."

"Christ."

At that moment Marlene Jory spotted Clint and disengaged herself from her father, who did not notice where she was going. The red-haired girl approached Clint and Leslie, and with her came Lucie Ellis, who was more incredible the closer she got.

"Mr. Adams," Marlene said. "How nice."

"Miss Jory."

"Oh, you'll have to call me Marlene, else how are we to be considered friends?"

"Whatever you say, Marlene. This is my partner, Frank Leslie."

"Nice to meet you, Mr. Leslie," she said. "This is my good friend Lucie Ellis. This is her father's house."

"Hello, Miss Ellis."

"Lucie," she said, putting her hand out. Surprised, Clint took her hand and held it, and she put her other hand over his and scratched the back of it with her nails. He felt heat rising in his groin and wondered how a girl that young could radiate that much sexuality.

"I'm afraid my father has warned me to stay away from you, Clint," Marlene Jory said.

Forcing his eyes away from those of Lucie Ellis, Clint looked at the older girl and said, "Really? I can't imagine why."

"Oh, I can," she said. "You said you were doing business with my father?"

"That's right."

"Then you must be getting the better of him."

"I'd say that at this point it was a standoff."

"You're being kind," she said, and was about to say

more when her father's voice called out, "Marlene!"

Clint looked past Marlene's head and saw her father approaching them in the company of another man. The other man was approximately the same age, though shorter and more portly than the banker.

"My dear," Jory said, touching her arm and ignoring both Clint and Frank Leslie, "your Uncle Wesley has been looking for you."

"Hello, Uncle Wesley," the girl said, giving the little man a fleeting peck on the cheek. "I was just talking to some of your guests. Have you met these gentlemen?"

"I'm afraid I, uh—" the mayor stammered.

"This is Clint Adams and Frank Leslie," she went on. "They own the Buckskin Saloon."

"Uh, yes, indeed," Mayor Ellis said. "Glad you could both come, gentlemen."

"Thanks for inviting us."

"Dear, I'd like you to come say hello to some of the other guests," Sherman Jory told his daughter.

"Oh, Father," she sighed. To Clint she said, "I'm afraid my father wants to show me off."

"And well he should," Clint replied.

"You're sweet," she said smiling. "I'm afraid I'll have to go away for a little while."

Before Clint could speak, Lucie Ellis grabbed his arm possessively and told Marlene Jory, "Don't worry, Marley, I'll take good care of Clint while you're gone."

"I'm sure you will," Marlene Jory said, and Clint was surprised at her tone. The two girls did not seem to be in competition with each other at all, and seemed to like each other very much. There was no hint of jealousy in Marlene Jory's tone.

"See you later," Marlene Jory told Clint, and she

went off with her father and Mayor Ellis, who was throwing apprehensive glances over his shoulder at his daughter.

"Would you like me to show you around?" Lucie Ellis asked Clint when the others had gone.

Clint looked at Frank Leslie, who shrugged his shoulders and said, "Don't let me stop you."

"Good," Lucie said, tugging on his arm. "Come on."

"Where are we going?" Clint asked.

"I want to show you the barn," she said.

"What's in the barn?"

"Hay," she said, and pulled him along harder.

When they entered the barn, Clint looked around and said, "Well, you were right. There is hay here. Now maybe we better get back to the—" he started to say, turning around, but he stopped short when he saw what she was doing.

First she had locked the doors from the inside, and then she had taken off her dress.

"Jesus," he said. Her breasts were tipped with large brown nipples that were already distended with excitement, and she had one hand between her legs, where the fingers were working feverishly.

"Uh, Lucie—"

"Ever since we were kids," she said, gasping, "Marley and I have been in friendly competition with each other. Now that she's back, from school, it's starting all over again—with you."

She threw her head back and pursed her lips, sucking in her breath as her fingers began moving faster and faster. Clint found himself the proud owner of a large, pulsing erection as he watched the girl work herself towards a frenzied orgasm.

"Jesus," he said, "I'm starting to feel left out."

She opened her eyes at that point and an extremely lewd, lascivious look invaded her lovely features.

"We can't have that," she said.

She walked up to Clint and began to unbuckle his belt. He took off his gunbelt and dropped it to the floor as she lowered his pants and dug out his raging erection.

"Oh, my, how pretty," she said. She fell to her knees and began to run her tongue over the head of his cock while cupping his scrotum in one hand. Suddenly, she opened her mouth and engulfed an amazing amount of him, squeezing his balls at the same time. Somewhat stunned by the turn of events, Clint found himself almost helpless in her hands . . . and mouth. His own hands reached to cup her head as it bobbed back and forth. She was working his tool with her lips, her tongue and her teeth with incredible expertise, bringing him right to the brink of explosion, and then abruptly releasing him.

"Your clothes," she gasped, and together they worked at removing all of them.

The top of her head barely came up to his chest, but she exhibited surprising strength as she pushed him back towards a stack of hay.

"Down, down" she was telling him. "Lie down."

He allowed her to push him down on his back, and she was as quick as a bunny, mounting him and engulfing him in her warm tunnel of love.

"Oooh," she crooned, grinding herself against him, "you fill me up!" She spread the length of her against him and began licking his nipples as she continued to move her hips.

Christ, now he thought he knew how a woman felt when she was being raped. Lucie was barely a handful, but she was in full charge of the moment, and he didn't feel a bit like fighting her. He reached around to cup her buttocks and hand rode her that way until she squealed that she was coming. At that moment, he let himself come, spurting his seed into her while she continued to ride him hard and dry him out.

She sat up on him, not allowing him to slide free, and reached behind her to tickle his balls, and then moved her fingers further down, to his anus. As she inserted one finger he felt his cock beginning to swell inside of her once again. Where did she learn all of this? he wondered, but he had not time to dwell on it because she was riding him wildly once again, bracing her hands against his flat stomach and jumping up and down on him shouting, "Deeper, deeper . . ."

He watched in fascination as her small, round breasts bounced about, then reached up to cup them in his hands and hold on while she rode them to another shattering climax . . . for both of them.

Satiated—if only for the moment—she lay down atop him and he put his arms around her, running his hands over her bare back and behind, enjoying the feel of her smooth ass cheeks against his palms.

"You haven't kissed me yet," she said into his ear.

"You haven't given me a chance," he replied.

She picked up her head and looked down at him with a crooked grin on her face. He brought one hand up to the back of her head and pulled her down to him. She opened her mouth and met his in a fierce, almost desperate kiss.

Chapter Nineteen

"Back so soon?" Frank Leslie asked sarcastically when Clint put in a reappearance at the barbecue.

"I think I'm ready to leave," Clint said.

"Why?"

"I'm a little tired."

"I can believe that," Leslie said. He looked past Clint and asked, "Where'd you leave her?"

"I didn't leave her, she left me," the Gunsmith said. "Oh, Jesus," he added, and Frank Leslie turned to see what had brought this response from his friend and saw Marlene Jory bearing down on them.

"Could I have a word with you, Clint?" she asked, then added, "If your friend doesn't mind?"

"Hell, I don't mind," Leslie said. "I'll just go amuse myself." He cast a sideways glance at Clint and said, "I've done that before."

Leslie went off and left Clint standing there with Marlene Jory, who latched onto his arm with both hands.

"Did she take you into the barn, that little scamp?"

"What?" he asked, not sure he had heard right.

"Lucie," Marlene said. "She took you into the barn, didn't she?"

"Did she tell you that?"

"She didn't have to," Marlene said, laughing. "I know Lucie better than anyone."

71

I'll bet, the Gunsmith thought.

"Besides, that's what I'd do if I could get away from my father long enough," she added, pressing her full breasts against his arm. "But as it is, we'll just have to wait until another time, won't we?"

"I suppose so," he replied.

"Oh, here comes Daddy. I better head him off. We'll see each other again, Clint. I promise."

She gave his arm a squeeze and rushed off to intercept her father.

Leslie came back and said to him, "We'll get out of here now . . . that is, if you can walk."

"Is it that obvious?"

"Not only is it obvious," Buckskin Frank said, "it's amazing, considering how long you were gone with Lucie. I'm very impressed, partner."

"Ah, shut up," Clint said. "I need a drink."

"They have a bar—"

"Not here. Jory's too busy showing off his daughter to try anything, and we're not getting anything accomplished by being here."

"I know I'm not, anyway," Leslie said.

Clint's raging erection had subsided somewhat and he said, "Come on, let's get out of here while I can still ride without crippling myself."

During the ride back Frank Leslie said, "I wouldn't exactly say we hadn't accomplished anything."

"If you're going to start in—"

"I'm not talking about you and Lucie," his partner said quickly, "but it does look like you might have a friend in Marlene Jory. If she really wants to be friends, you might be able to get advance information out of her about what tricks her father has up his sleeve."

"You think she'd help us?"

"Why not?" Leslie asked. "We're not trying to hurt her father, we're just trying to keep our business. Once we make the rest of the payments, there won't be anything Jory can do, anyway. Keep it in mind, Clint. If she wants you to, uh, service her, just consider it an additional donation to the cause."

Clint thought about servicing Marlene Jory, and that made him think about Lucie Ellis . . . .

Shifting about on his saddle, trying to find a more comfortable position, he said, "Can we talk about something else for a while?"

Leslie laughed and abruptly slapped Duke on the rump, causing him to take off at a gallop, bouncing Clint about painfully.

"You bastard!"

When they got back to town they returned their horses to the livery and walked over to the saloon. Business seemed respectable, and Joy was behind the bar and nodded at them when they came in.

When they reached the bar Clint said, "Joy, how about two beers."

"You're back early," she said, setting two beer mugs before them. "How was the bash?"

"Exhausting," Clint said.

"For some of us," Leslie added with a smirk.

Clint gave him a dirty look and picked up his beer. He drained it and told Leslie, "Why don't you relieve Joy behind the bar, Frank. I'm going to go upstairs and take a hot bath."

"That'll relax your muscle—I mean, your muscles," Leslie told him, grinning from ear to ear.

Leaning her elbows on the bar and showing some impressive cleavage Joy asked, "And why do his muscles need relaxing?"

Clint looked at her and said, "It's a long story, Joy."

"I've got time."

Now he gave Frank Leslie the eye and said, "Frank, why don't you tell her. I'll be down to relieve you in a little while."

"Sure, Clint," Leslie said, magnanimously. "Enjoy your soak."

As he made for the stairs he heard her asking Leslie the same question again, and he hoped his partner would be able to come up with a good answer.

Later that day Sherman Jory met with Martin Cort in his office at the bank.

"Martin, I've decided to do things your way."

"How is that, Mr. Jory?"

"I'm going to use more force," Jory said.

"What changed your mind?"

"My daughter is interested in Clint Adams," the banker explained. "I've warned her to stay away from him, but she's a very strong-willed girl—which, if you'll remember, was the reason I sent her east in the first place."

"I remember," Cort said.

"By warning her away I've played right into her hands."

Martin Cort remembered Marlene Jory as a sixteen and seventeen year old little tease. He had tried to bed her on several occasions, but she had always turned him away—the little bitch!

"You want me to take care of them, then?" Cort asked, touching his gun.

"No, not yet," Jory said. "I'm going to bring in some outside help on this."

"Who?"

"I'll do a little research into that before I decide," Jory said. "You know how much I know about gunmen. I want somebody who is good."

"I've told you before, Mr. Jory," Cort said, standing up and leaning on the older man's desk. "I can take them, both of them."

"And you may get your chance, Martin," Jory replied. "But not until I say so."

"Then why bring someone else in?"

"Because I want to make sure it gets done right," Jory said, standing up himself, looking at some point past Martin Cort's ear. "I not only want that saloon, I want both of those men out of town—or dead."

Chapter Twenty

Sheriff Tom Sideman was seated in his office leafing through some new wanted posters when half of the Gold-dust pain-in-the-butt twins walked into his office.

Between Sherman Jory and Mayor Wesley Ellis, they managed to make at least a small part of each day a painful experience. This morning, the day after the barbecue, it was Sherman Jory, the banker.

"Good morning, Sheriff."

"Good morning, Mr. Jory," Sideman said, resignedly, not bothering to look up from his posters.

"I have some business to take up with you, Sheriff," Jory told the lawman.

"I'm listening, Mr. Jory," Sideman answered, still not looking at the banker.

"I wish you would look at me when I'm speaking to you, sir," Jory said gruffly.

Sideman closed his eyes, took a deep breath, let it out, then looked at Jory and said, "What is it, Mr. Jory?"

"I must say, your attitude is less than courteous, considering my standing in this town."

"Is that what you came here to tell me?" Sideman asked. "That you don't like my attitude?"

"Not at all, although I'm sure I'll take that specific point up with the town council at a later date."

"I'm sure you will."

"My current business concerns the Buckskin Saloon."

"What about the saloon?"

"It is not actually the saloon itself, but the men who run it."

"Frank Leslie?"

"And Clint Adams."

"Could we get to the point, Mr. Jory?" Sideman asked. "What about them?"

"They're both gunfighters, Sheriff," Jory said. "We certainly don't need their kind in Brightwater."

"They haven't bothered anyone, Mr. Jory, and they're certainly doing a good business there. I haven't had any complaints about them from anyone else."

"Well, I'm sure you will, unless you do something to get rid of them."

"Mr. Jory, I have no reason to run either man out of town, and I have no intention of doing so just to please you."

"Mayor Ellis—"

"Or to please Mayor Ellis," Sideman said, interrupting the banker. "Now, if you'll excuse me, I have work to do."

"Are you sure there are no wanted posters on either of these men?" Jory demanded.

"Well, if there is, and I come across it, I'll arrest them."

"I'd like to look at some posters."

"I'm afraid I won't allow that, Mr. Jory. I don't come into your bank demanding to look at your records. Good day."

Jory fumed, incensed that this ex-schoolteacher should treat him this way.

"You're letting that star go to your head, schoolteacher," he said tightly.

"Mr. Jory," Sideman said without looking up, "I suggest you get out of my office before I throw you out."

"You'll regret this, Sideman."

"Take it up with the town council."

Chapter Twenty-One

During Clint's shift behind the bar that night Sheriff Sideman came in for a drink.

"Evenin', Sheriff," Clint greeted. "What can I get for you?"

"Just a beer, Adams."

"Coming up."

Clint brought the beer over and the lawman said, "I don't mind telling you, Adams, you surprised me."

"I did? How's that?"

"I didn't figure you to be around this long."

"Why not? Brightwater seems like a nice, quiet little town, a nice place to settle."

"Your kind doesn't settle down, Adams. You know that."

Clint bit back his initial remark and instead asked, "Is that based on your many years of experience?"

"All right," Sideman conceded, "so I still know more about teaching school than I do about being a lawman, but I'm learning."

"On the job," Clint pointed out. "That can be pretty dangerous—and it would be, in any other town but one like Brightwater."

"I can handle myself," Sideman said.

"Sure you can," Clint said, and then added to himself, *in a classroom full of kids*.

"You seem to have made an enemy or two since you've been here, though," Sideman told Clint.

"Like who?"

"I had a visit from Sherman Jory this morning," Sideman said after taking a sip from his beer. "Seems he wants me to run you and your partner out of town."

"That's not surprising."

"Mind telling me why?"

"If we default on our payments, he takes over the saloon."

"You mean the bank does."

"The bank or Jory, it amounts to the same thing. He ends up with the business. I'm sure he's picked up a few other businesses the same way."

"Jory is supposed to be on the up and up," Sideman said. "Are you telling me that he's using his position in the bank to take over businesses in Brightwater?"

"Somebody shot up our whiskey shipment, and without that whiskey we couldn't have made enough money to meet this month's payment."

"That doesn't mean it's Sherman Jory—not that I like the man or wouldn't believe the worst about him, but I couldn't act without some kind of physical evidence."

"Hey, you are learning aren't you?" Clint said. "We're not asking you to act, Sheriff. We'll take care of that ourselves."

"Don't break the law in my town, Adams," Sideman warned.

"I have no intention of breaking the law, Sheriff," Clint assured the lawman, "but I also have no intention of letting anyone take over my business."

"I'm sorry," the sheriff said, setting down his empty beer mug, "but I can't seem to see the Gunsmith as a businessman."

"Maybe I can do something to change your mind."

"Just don't do anything to make me change mine."

"What does that mean, exactly?"

"I told Jory that I had no reason to try and run you or your partner out of Brightwater, so please don't do anything to make me change my mind."

Chapter Twenty-Two

With the reappearance of his daughter, Marlene, Sherman Jory had to discontinue the late night visits of Lila Shore, which did not make him happy. Nor did seeing Clint Adams go into the barn with Lucie Ellis. That just gave him one more reason for wanting Adams gone . . . or dead.

So, as pleased as he was to see his daughter, her presence did pose some problems. Lila Shore—or access to any of the whores from Kelly's—was one problem, and his meetings with Martin Cort were the other. Marlene made sure that her father knew how much she disliked Cort, so he intended to keep the man as far away from her as possible. That meant that all of their business would have to be done in his office at the bank.

"First time I've been in a bank late at night," Martin Cort said as he was admitted by Jory. "Any chance of picking up some samples?"

"I'm sure that was meant to be funny, but the humor escapes me," Jory said. "Come into my office."

Cort followed his employer into the office and closed the door behind them.

"I tried to get a look at some wanted posters in the sheriff's office today, but I failed," Jory said.

"Why wanted posters?" Cort asked, and when Jory

didn't answer right away he said, "Wait a minute. You wanted to look through wanted posters for a gunman?"

"All right, so I went about it the wrong way."

"Those men are wanted because nobody can find them," Cort explained. "How did you expect to?"

"Do you have any ideas?"

Suddenly, a crafty look came over Cort's face, but he masked it quickly.

"I might," Cort said. "If you're really serious about bringing in a gunman, I could probably find someone faster than you could."

"Then do it!"

"It will probably cost you a bundle."

"For you, or him?"

Cort shrugged and said, "For both. In fact, if I can get the man I have in mind, there'll be more than one, because he works with partners."

"If it will get rid of these two men, I'll pay it," Jory said.

"I'll take care of it, then," Cort said, standing up. "How is your daughter, by the way? She certainly has grown up in two years."

"Stay away from my daughter, Cort," Jory said, his tone suddenly menacing.

"I'm not good enough for her?"

"That's an understatement, but beyond that she detests you."

"I don't have to take that," Cort growled.

"For the amount of money you are planning to take me for, you'll take whatever I give you. Stay away from my daughter."

Jory wished he could also order the man away from Lucie Ellis, but that would look suspicious.

Cort shook with suppressed rage, and it was the thought of the money that finally enabled him to control himself. *First I'll take your money*, he thought, *and then, old man, I'll take your daughter.*

When Cort left the bank he headed for Kelly's. Normally, he would have gone to his cabin, where Lucie Ellis would be waiting for him, but Lucie had been curiously distant with him since the barbecue, and he didn't know why. She had refused to meet him that evening, giving him some phony excuse. She must have been seeing someone else, and although Cort didn't like the idea, he decided not to let it bother him that much. There were plenty of whores over at Kelly's and there was that one—Lila—that even looked a little like Lucie.

Especially if he gave it to her from behind.

Chapter Twenty-Three

"Are you sure he won't come here tonight?" Marlene Jory asked Lucie Ellis.

"What for? I told him I wouldn't be here. He'll probably go over to Kelly's. We won't be disturbed."

"Good. It's time we caught up with each other. Tell me how Clint Adams was," Marley asked.

"Oh, he was incredible, Marley," Lucie answered.

"Is he big?" Marlene asked.

"And long," Lucie said. "I felt like his thing was all the way up here," she said, touching the space between her small breasts.

"Really?" Marlene asked. "I had a teacher in school like that."

"You went to bed with one of your teachers?"

"Well, we never really went to bed. He was married, and he never had enough money for a hotel."

"So where did you do it?" Lucie asked.

"On his desk, after class."

"On his desk!" Lucie said, eyes widening. "What if you had gotten caught?"

"Lucie," Marlene said, "that just added to the excitement."

Lucie thought about that for a while, and said, "I guess it would."

"Remember now," Marlene said, "it's my turn with him next."

"Well, hurry up," Lucie said, "because I can't wait to do it with him again."

"What about Martin Cort?"

"I'm tired of Martin."

"I don't know what you ever saw in him, anyway," Marlene said. "He disgusts me."

"Well, I couldn't do it with any of the hands on Father's ranch. Martin was just available."

"I guess when you get the itch you take whatever's available," Marlene said, understanding.

"Which one of us do you think Clint will like the best?" Lucie asked.

"Me, of course," Marlene said.

"Why you?"

"Because darling," Marlene said, "I can help him get the best of my father."

Chapter Twenty-Four

"I wonder just how many businesses Sherman Jory does own in this town?" Clint asked aloud at breakfast the next morning.

"It must be more than a few," Frank Leslie said. "How would we find out, though? Go around and ask people, 'Are you working for Sherman Jory'?"

"There are other ways," Clint said.

"Sure. We can ask Jory himself."

"No, I had someone else in mind to ask."

"Oh, who?"

"Miss Jesse Wells."

"The girl who works at the bank?" Leslie asked. "The nice girl you told me about?"

"That's the one."

"How do you figure to get that close to a nice girl that she'll talk about her boss?"

Pouring himself another cup of coffee, Clint said, "I'll just be nice to her."

"Okay, let's say we find out how many businesses he owns. What do we do with the information then?"

"I don't know," Clint answered. "Let's get the information first, and then worry about what we'll do with it."

"Okay, partner," Leslie said, "but I guess I'll just have to wait until you come up with the information before I can get actively involved."

"Hey, if you want to try your hand with Miss Wells—"

"Oh, no," Leslie begged off, "I've never been much of a hand with good girls, Clint."

"Well, after Joy and Lucie Ellis—not to mention Marlene Jory—I just hope I remember how to treat someone who's—who's—"

"Innocent?"

"That's the word."

"It's more than a word," Leslie said. "You can't treat her the way you treat Joy—"

"What about the way I treat Joy?"

"She watches every move you make, Clint, and you haven't been paying that much attention to her, anymore."

"I never knew a whore to get emotionally involved with someone, but that's what I felt happening, so I backed off."

"For good?" Buckskin Frank asked, sounding a little anxious.

"Yeah, Frank, for good," Clint said. Was he imagining it, or was Frank Leslie more than just a little concerned about Joy. "Why?"

"Uh, no reason. She's just a nice kid, that's all."

"She's no kid . . . but I know what you mean," Clint said. "All right, so I'm going to have to forget about Joy, Lucie, Marlene and whoever and concentrate on Jesse Wells. If we can get something on banker Jory, we can get him off our backs and run our business."

"That's an awful lot to forget about," Leslie said. "You have my sympathies."

"Thanks a lot. Another beer?"

"I don't think so. I think I'll just, uh, see you later," Leslie said. "I'll relieve you."

He backed away from the bar, looked uncertain about which way he wanted to go, and then left the saloon.

Clint felt that his partner might have been experiencing some feelings he wasn't prepared to deal with, but then the Gunsmith had his own feelings to handle.

He was starting to feel itchy, to feel like moving on, but he couldn't do that until things were right with Frank Leslie and the Buckskin Saloon.

He had bought his way into this hand, and now he had to play it out.

And his ace in the hole might just turn out to be Miss Jesse Wells.

Frank Leslie thought a turn around town in the fresh air might clear some of the cobwebs from his head. Never much of a ladies' man, he had nevertheless been having some thoughts about Joy Darling, now that Clint no longer seemed interested. He only hoped that the same would apply to Joy's feelings for Clint.

Then there were his own feelings about the saloon. Sooner or later, things were going to start to get pretty rough—if Sherman Jory wanted the saloon that badly. The question in Frank Leslie's mind was, did he want it as bad?

Was he wrong to think that someone like him—or like the Gunsmith—could settle down in a nice, small town and run a business. Would people allow them to do that?

As Frank Leslie turned a corner to walk down one of Brightwater's less busy streets, he found out that there was at least one person in town who wouldn't allow it.

That was the person who chose that moment to put a bullet in Buckskin Frank Leslie's back.

Chapter Twenty-Five

"How is he?" The Gunsmith asked the doctor.

Dr. Greg Tobin held up a small, misshapen piece of lead and said, "Well, I got the bullet out of his back, now the rest is up to him."

Shot in the back! The words flashed through the Gunsmith's mind again and again. When he heard the shot that morning, it was as if he instinctively knew what had happened. Filled with dread he ran down the street and broke through the crowd that had surrounded the fallen Frank Leslie who, with his face in the dirt, looked more dead than alive. He immediately picked up his friend and rushed to the doctor's office with him, rather than wait for someone to summon the doctor to the scene.

Now, standing there examining the bullet in the doctor's hand, those words flashed through his mind again. *Shot in the back*—just like Bill Hickok.

Sherman Jory would pay for this. Clint was sure that the banker had not fired the shot himself, but he was behind it, of that he had no doubt, and he would pay dearly—especially if Frank died.

"When will we know if he'll . . . pull through?"

"It will take a while, Mr. Adams," the young physician said. "There's really no need for you to stay and wait. I'll let you know as soon as I know something. I promise."

"Thanks, Doc," Clint said. "I've got to go and talk to the sheriff, anyway. After that I'll be at the Buckskin Saloon. Why don't you come by for a drink later, on the house?"

"Thank you, I might do that," Dr. Tobin said, "but not until my patient is stable."

"I appreciate that, Doctor. I'll take care of all the expenses."

"Don't worry about that now, Mr. Adams. You go and do what you have to do."

"That's one piece of advice I intend to take, Doctor."

As Clint left the doctor's office, Tobin felt extremely sorry for whoever had shot Frank Leslie, if and when Clint Adams caught up to him.

Clint went straight to Sheriff Sideman's office but found a deputy instead of the sheriff.

"Can I help you?" the deputy asked.

"I was looking for the sheriff."

"He's out investigating a shooting," the deputy replied. "Maybe I can help you?"

The deputy was a man in his late thirties, and had the demeanor of an experienced man.

"My name is Adams. The man who was shot is my partner."

"You're Clint Adams," the deputy stated.

"That's right."

"Yeah, the sheriff mentioned that you had become partner in the Buckskin Saloon."

"That's right," Clint said, then added, "I haven't seen you in there, have I?"

"Uh, no, you haven't," the deputy admitted. "I do my drinking at the Brightwater."

"You should give us a try," Clint said. "We can use the business."

"Maybe I will. Is there anything you'd like me to tell the sheriff when he gets back?"

"No, I think I'll talk to him later." Clint was about to leave when a thought struck him. "What's your name, Deputy? You know mine, which puts me at a disadvantage."

"I'm Steve Owen."

Clint took three steps forward and shook hands with the deputy.

"How long have you been a deputy, Steve?"

"More'n ten years, now. Before that I was in the Army for a spell," the man answered.

"You've got a lot of experience then."

"Some."

"What do you think of Sheriff Sideman?"

"He's got a lot to learn, but he's doing the best job he knows how," Owen said. "He cares about what he's doing, too."

"I guess he leans on you for advice, huh?"

"Advice, yeah, sometimes, but he makes his own decisions. If you're worried, he'll do the best job he can of finding out who killed your partner."

"I believe you, Steve. Thanks for being frank with me."

"Want me to tell him you were by?"

"Sure, but I'll stop by again later, anyway."

"Okay." As Clint walked to the door the deputy called out, "Mr. Adams."

"Yeah?"

"It was a real pleasure meeting you."

Clint nodded and said, "Well, if that's true, call me Clint next time I'm by."

Going out the door he thought of adding, *Just as long as you don't call me the Gunsmith.*

Chapter Twenty-Six

Clint went back to the saloon and relieved Joy behind the bar.

"How is he?" she asked with great concern.

"The doctor got the bullet out, but beyond that we don't know anything for sure, yet." He took a glass from beneath the bar and poured himself a shot of whiskey.

"Do you know who did it?"

"Yeah," he said. "A coward." Clint pried his eyes out of his glass. "No, we don't know who did it, Joy. He was shot in the back."

"Oh, how horrible. Did you talk to the sheriff?"

"I tried, but he's out investigating the shooting, according to Steve Owen."

"Do you want me to stay behind the bar for a while?"

"Yeah, why don't you? I've got some things I have to do." He finished his drink and capped the whiskey bottle.

"Clint, don't get into trouble," she warned.

"There's trouble brewing, Joy," he said, "and I didn't start it."

"You're gonna finish it, huh?"

"I just want to find out who backshot my partner."

"And kill him?"

"No," he replied quickly, and then again, "No."

"What was it an amorous cowboy once told me?" she said. "Your lips say no, but your eyes say—"

"Tend bar," he told her.

"Yes, boss."

He left the saloon wondering what he would do if he found the man in the next few hours, before he could fully cool off. He wouldn't want to kill him, but visions of Frank Leslie lying in the dirt—not to mention Bill Hickok, lying on a saloon floor—would not make it easy to resist.

Going over to the Brightwater bank he presented himself to Miss Jesse Wells.

"Jesse, I'd like to see Mr. Jory."

"I would have to see if he's busy—"

"I tell you what," Clint said, starting past her desk. "I'll check for you."

"Mr. Adams—" she started, but he was already going through Jory's office door and slammed it behind him.

The man behind the desk jerked his head up and stared at Clint, wide-eyed.

"What the hell do you think—"

"My partner is lying near death with a bullet hole in his back," Clint said, and the rage he was feeling was plainly evident in his voice.

"Why come to me—" Jory started to say, pushing his chair back until it bumped into the wall.

"Because," Clint said, leaning over Jory's desk, "if I find out you had anything to do with it, I'm going to come after you, Jory, and there isn't going to be anywhere you can run."

"That's a threat!"

"It sure is, friend, and you better remember it."

"You can't threaten me—" Jory said, starting to get up out of his chair, but Clint placed his hand flat against the man's chest and shoved him back into it so hard that the chair almost turned over from Jory's considerable bulk.

"You can't—"

"I can, and I will, Jory, and you better remember it."

He left the bankman pinned there against the wall, and hoped that he was feeling apprehensive about his immediate future.

Chapter Twenty-Seven

Clint went back to the saloon to relieve Joy for a few hours; then he was going to check at the sheriff's office to see if Sideman was back. He saw Deputy Steve Owen enter and approach the bar and said, "I didn't expect you to take me up on my invitation so soon, Steve. What'll you have?"

"I didn't come here for a drink, Clint," the deputy said. "I came to get you."

"Get me? For what?"

"The sheriff would like to see you in his office."

"Now?"

"Five minutes ago. Have you got somebody here who can cover for you?"

"Yeah, sure," Clint said. He caught Joy's eye and waved her over.

"Hello, Steve," she said, coming up next to the deputy. "Long time no see."

"Hello, Joy."

"Joy, can you cover the bar? I've got to go over and see the sheriff," Clint explained, then looked at Deputy Owen and added, "By special invitation."

"Sure, Clint," she said, switching places with him. To Owen she said, "Come around once in a while, Steve. It's nice to see a familiar face."

Clint noticed the tone of her voice and looked at her, wondering if she were going to start selling it again.

The two men left the saloon together and crossed the street, and Clint asked, "Let me guess. The sheriff had a visit from our very respectable banker, Sherman Jory."

"Mr. Jory did come by a little while ago. Did you go to see him?"

"We had a talk, yeah," he said, admitting to himself even before this that it hadn't been one of his better ideas.

"Yeah," the deputy said, and they entered the sheriff's office.

"Make your rounds, Steve," Sideman instructed his deputy.

"Sure, Sheriff."

Sideman waited until his man had left and then said, "Sit down, Adams."

Clint did as he was told and asked, "What have you found out about my partner's shooting?"

"First things first," Sideman said. "Whatever possessed you to bust into Sherman Jory's office and make threats against one of this town's leading citizens?"

Clint's mouth dropped open and then he demanded, "Is that what you call first things first, Sheriff?" He stood up and added, "I guess I must have been wrong about you."

"Sit down, Clint."

They locked eyes and Clint very slowly lowered himself back into the chair.

"Okay," Sideman said after a moment. "Nobody knows anything about your partner being shot. Everybody heard the shot, but nobody saw anything."

"Where was Jory?" Clint asked.

"I didn't have a chance to ask him!" Sideman exploded. "I was too busy listening to him complain about you. He wants me to lock you up, Adams."

"Sure he does," Clint said. "With my partner near death and me in jail, he's free to add one more business to his collection."

"You haven't shown me any proof that what you say about Jory is true, so let's not go into that right now, okay?"

"Are you?"

"Am I what?"

"Going to lock me up."

Looking very annoyed with himself Sideman said, "No, I'm not going to lock you up . . . just yet."

"That must have made a big hit with Jory."

"Well, he made certain threats about my job, but he's been making threats for a long time."

"I see. Then I'm free to go."

"Yes—but stay away from Jory."

"I can't do that, Sheriff," Clint said, standing up. "He's the one responsible for my partner getting shot—"

"You don't know that."

"I do."

"No, you don't, Adams. Leslie has a reputation, remember? It could have been anyone who pulled that trigger."

"If you keep believing that, Sheriff, you're not going to be much use to me."

"Oh, really? I'm not much help to you?" Sideman asked, and now he stood up. "I'll tell you what, Adams. You bring me some kind of evidence on Sherman Jory, and then maybe I can be of more help to you. All right?"

Chapter Twenty-Eight

From the sheriff's office Clint went to the doctor's office to check on Leslie's condition.

"How is he, Doc?" he said without preamble.

"He's no worse, which is encouraging."

"That means he's no better, right?"

"I'm afraid not," Tobin answered. "He's very fortunate that the bullet entered high up on his left side. It missed his heart."

"That is lucky. Has he regained consciousness?"

"Not yet. Do you think he'll know who shot him?"

"No, I don't. It's pretty obvious that he was shot from behind. I don't think he saw who shot him."

"Then how do you propose to find out?"

"Just ask questions, I guess," Clint answered, then he looked at the doctor and said, "What makes you think I'm going to try and find out?"

"He is your partner, Mr. Adams, and I must say that your reputation precedes you."

"I see."

"If I can do anything to help, please let me know. I detest this sort of cowardice."

"So do I," Clint replied. "You can keep me informed about his condition."

"Of course."

"I'd like to talk to him as soon as possible, just in case he does know something."

"Rest assured, I will keep you informed."

"Thank you, Doctor."

Clint went back to the saloon, but when he reached it he kept walking until he reached the street where Frank Leslie had been shot. He walked to the exact spot, but there was no evidence there that it had ever happened.

He looked around, but the street was still deserted. It was a side street, and the only windows that looked onto it were second or third floor windows. Whoever had shot him would have had to do it from one of those windows, or while standing in the street right behind him. Clint figured that the kind of man who would shoot another in the back would not have done it standing out in plain sight, so that meant it was done from one of the windows.

Standing in the spot where Leslie had been when fired upon, Clint picked out three of the more likely windows and decided to check them out. Two of the windows were hotel rooms and a third was a room over the general store. Clint decided to check the general store first, and as he turned to the corner to do so, he walked right into Sheriff Tom Sideman.

"Don't you have a business to run?" Sideman asked the Gunsmith.

"Yes, I do, but I was just out taking a walk—"

"To the general store?"

"What makes you say that?"

"Adams, I just checked the room over the store that looks out onto the street where Leslie was shot. The owner of the store was behind the counter, and he says no one could have gone up there without his knowledge."

"What about a back door?"

"You need a key for that, and he has the only one."

"I see."

"Now I'm going over to the hotel to check the rooms on that side of the building—and I don't need any help!"

"All right, don't get so upset, Sheriff. I'm not trying to do your job."

"Oh, no? Then just whose job are you trying to do?"

"Mine!" Clint shot back. "When a man's partner is backshot, damn it, it's his job to find out who did it."

"You're not a lawman anymore, Adams, and this is a job for the law!"

Clint did not want to stand toe to toe with the sheriff right in the middle of town and argue, so he said, "You win, Sheriff. I'll go back to my saloon and take care of business."

"Fine, you do that, and I'll take care of my business," Sideman replied. "See how easy it is to get along when we both know our place?"

"Sure. Why right now, we're almost as close as brothers, aren't we?"

As Clint started to walk past Sideman, the sheriff stopped him and said, "Your saloon is that way," pointing in the opposite direction.

"I know where my saloon is, Sheriff, but I need some coffee and sugar from the general store. Good luck with your investigation, and I'd appreciate it if you would keep me informed."

"Sure, right after I talk to the mayor and the town council, I'll come running right over to you."

"That's right nice of you, Sheriff."

Muttering to himself, the ex-schoolteacher brushed past Clint and headed for the hotel. When he was out of sight, Clint went into the general store to talk to the owner himself.

Everything the sheriff had told him was repeated to

him by the owner, Sam Jackson, who had been into the Buckskin Saloon on more than one occasion. Clint had a feeling that he might have been a regular customer of Joy's while she was at Kelly's, and had followed her to the Buckskin in hopes of continuing their business relationship.

"So there's no way anyone could have gotten up there without being seen by you."

"That's what I told the sheriff, and that's what I'm telling you," Jackson said. He was a slightly built man in his early forties, with a weak chin and wire frame spectacles.

"And you have the only key."

"Well . . . yeah, I've got the only key . . . that counts," the man said.

"That counts?" Clint asked, frowning. "What does that mean, the only one that counts? You mean there is another key?"

"Well, there is, but—look, I can't talk about that."

"What do you mean you can't talk about that?" Clint demanded. "If there's another key then that means that someone could have used it to get in through the back door and up to that room."

"No, they couldn't," Jackson said. "It belongs to . . . to someone who wouldn't use it."

"Who?" Clint asked. "Who does it belong to, Mr. Jackson?"

"I'm not supposed to—uh, I have a partner, and he has a key, but he never comes here—"

"Who is he?"

"I can't say, Mr. Adams," the little man said. "He's a silent partner. He don't have nothing to do with the way the store's run."

"I see. A silent partner, and you can't mention his name."

"That's right."

"Well, then I won't push you for it," Clint said, backing off. He backed off because he had a notion about who the silent partner might be, and he didn't want Jackson running back to the man and mentioning their conversation.

"I knew you'd understand, Mr. Adams," Jackson said, gratefully.

"Sure, I understand. Mr. Jackson, would you mind if I went upstairs and took a look around?"

"The sheriff already done that."

"I know, but I'd like to have a look for myself, if it's all right with you."

"Sure, go ahead. Door's back there."

"Thanks."

Clint went through the door Jackson had indicated, and found a small hallway with a stairway and, further down, the locked back door. He checked the door and found it locked, and then went up the stairs to the second floor. There were a couple of rooms up there, but he found the one he wanted and closed the door behind him. Staring out the window he could see very clearly the street and the spot where Leslie had been shot. He could also see Sheriff Tom Sideman in one of the rooms across the street, so he ducked back away from the window and began examining the floor. He didn't find anything, but then his mind wasn't really on what he was seeing, it was on what Sam Jackson had told him, and had probably not told the sheriff.

Clint felt sure that the silent partner was Sherman Jory, and that the general store was another of the businesses that he had swallowed up, using his position in the bank. Maybe this piece of information would be his first step in convincing the sheriff that what he said about Sherman Jory was true. He had no doubt that the town of Brightwater would be much better off without banker Jory, and he hoped to be able to do something about that very soon.

He left the general store, once again thanking Sam Jackson for talking to him. Stepping out of the store he saw the sheriff leaving the hotel, and he stepped back in and waited a few moments, in order to avoid confronting the lawman again. Once the coast was clear, he left and headed for the saloon.

He went right to the bar and told Joy, "I'm just going to go upstairs for a minute, and then I'll be down to relieve you."

"That's okay," she assured him. "I'm handling it. Take your time. Did you find out anything?"

"Frank's condition is still the same," he said. "The doctor will let me know if there's any change."

She nodded and said, "Why don't you go upstairs and get some rest, okay?"

"Sure. I'll be down in a while."

He went upstairs, and when he entered his room he realized that he must have been more tired than he thought, because he entered without the hint that there was someone inside waiting for him.

It was Marlene Jory. She was sitting up in his bed with the covers held up to her neck, and she smiled as he entered.

"Marlene."

"Hello, Clint."

"How did you get up here?"

Using her eyes she indicated the window and said, "I climbed in the window."

"The window. That was kind of dangerous, don't you think? You could have gotten hurt."

"I was a tomboy," she told him. "I know all about climbing trees and such."

"You do, huh? You don't look like a tomboy right now, I can tell you that."

"Why, thank you, sir."

"Would you like to tell me what was so important that you had to risk your neck climbing up here?" he asked—as if he didn't already know.

"I brought you something."

"What?"

"These," she said, and dropped the covers to her waist.

Chapter Twenty-Nine

She cupped her large, naked breasts in her hands and flicked her thumbs across the rosy colored nipples until they were standing at attention.

"Do you like them?" she asked.

"Very much," he answered, very aware of the heat that was building up in his groin. The girl had an absolutely stunning pair of breasts, there was no denying that.

"Lucie has a cute little body, don't you think?" she said, then added, "But there's nothing like a nice, big pair of tits—with big nipples just begging for a man's mouth . . . and tongue . . . and teeth . . ."

She raised her eyebrows at him, licked her lips and looked at him expectantly. She continued to run her fingertips along the deep undersides of her breasts.

"You're incredible," he finally said.

"Well, that's a start," she admitted. "Why don't you come over here and we can get started."

"You look like you're doing pretty good on your own," he observed.

"Oh, no," she said. "It doesn't matter how good I can make myself feel, there's nothing like having a man in bed with me"—She closed her eyes and began running her hands over her body as she continued— "putting his hands on me . . . his mouth . . . driving into me . . ."

He had never seen or heard anything as erotic as this

healthy young creature fondling herself, talking about what she wanted a man to do to her.

Unbuckling his gunbelt he asked, "Am I correct in assuming that you would like me to get in that bed with you?"

"Oh, yes, Mr. Adams. I definitely want you in this bed with me. The sooner, the better."

There was no denying his need at that moment, so he didn't think twice about undressing and approaching the bed.

"Oh, my," she said, staring at his crotch. "You are ready, aren't you?"

"As ready as you are, I think," he said huskily.

He was about to get on the bed when she said, "Stop."

"Changing your mind?" he asked. "I don't mind telling you it's too late for that."

"You'd force me?"

"I'd only have to touch you and you'd force me," he said. "Your body is crying out for a man's touch at this very moment, and I'm the only man in the room, right now."

"You're right about that," she said, "and I'm not changing my mind. I just want you to stand there for a few moments while we get better acquainted."

With that she reached out and took his swollen penis in her hand, squeezing it lovingly. "I'm about to show you some of those things I learned back East."

"And some of the ones you already knew before you left, I'm sure."

She laughed—an incredibly lewd, sexy sound—slid off the bed and assumed a position on her knees before him. Letting his erection rest in the palm of her hand, she opened her mouth and engulfed the tip and then, very slowly, began to draw more and more of the organ into her mouth. She took enough of it in so that her erect nipples were pressed up against his thighs. She enjoyed the way the hair on his thighs tickled her nipples and she began to brush them back and forth against him as she sucked on him.

His hands moved by themselves to cup the back of her head as time and again she brought him to the brink of orgasm.

"Mmm," she said when she finally allowed him to pop free from her mouth, "that's how they do it back East."

"Well," he said, putting his hands under her arms and lifting her up, "let me show how we do it here in the West."

He lifted her off her feet and dropped her onto the bed, and before she could bounce a second time he was on top of her. The first thing he wanted were those incredible breasts, and he tried to cover every inch of them with his mouth at one time. He sucked on the nipples until she was moaning and thrashing beneath him, and then he kissed and nipped his way down to the downy red growth between her legs. He tasted her with his tongue, thrusting it in and out of her; then he found her clit and nibbled on it until she was bouncing the both of them up and down on the bed.

"Ooh, give it to me, please, give it to me now . . ." she moaned, and he raised himself up and plunged into her as far as he could go.

"Oh, God, you're driving me wild!" she cried out. "Do it harder and harder . . . oooh, yes, yes, that's it, that's the way . . ."

Her opulent curves felt wonderful beneath him, quite different from the way Lucie Ellis's smaller body felt. Each had her own special attractions, and Marlene's were very evident at the moment.

"I've got you," she said, exerting pressure around him, sucking on him, wrapping her strong, heavy thighs around him. "I've got you, now."

He cupped her buttocks in his hands and deliberately slowed down the tempo, to show her who really had who.

"Oh, God, faster, please," she whispered, "I need it . . . faster . . ."

"Well, you'll get it the way I want to give it to you," he told her.

"Ooh, you want to be in control, don't you, Mr. Adams?" she asked, running her nails over his back.

He kneaded her buttocks as he drove into her and she alternately closed and rolled her eyes, biting her lip until a spot of blood appeared, which he immediately licked away.

"God," she said, and latched onto his tongue with her teeth, gently sucking it into her mouth.

The time was very rapidly approaching, for both of them, and again Clint began to increase the tempo of his thrusts, until they were thrusting at each other over and over again, grunting and groaning in a wild kind of abandon, until her body was wracked by shudders, and then he was emptying into her, only there seemed to be no end to it, and the more he spurted into her, the more she seemed to suck from him, until he was utterly drained.

"God," she said, her breath coming raggedly. "When East meets West they really explode, don't they?"

Chapter Thirty

As he dressed later she said, "Do you really have to go?"

"Yes," he replied, "and so do you, the same way you came, I'm afraid."

"You didn't ask me why I came," she said, sliding from the bed and starting to dress. He stopped to watch as, big breasts swaying, she pulled on her skirt.

"I thought you made that pretty clear."

"That?" she asked, looking at the bed. "That was for fun, and I'd like to do it again, real soon." She put on her blouse and began to button it. "No, I came here to help you."

"Help me with what?"

"You said you were in business with my father," she recounted. "That can only mean that you're up against him. He's a vicious businessman. I can help you."

"Why should you? After all, he is your father."

"An accident of birth," she said, and for a moment he saw the bitterness that lay just beneath the surface. "What he did to my mother a father would never do," she finished, and offered no further explanation. She pulled on her boots and walked to the window, where she turned to face him again. "I'll be around, if you decide you need my help . . . or simply need me."

"I'll let you know, Marlene," Clint said, "and thank you."

"Oh, thank *you,*" she said, smiling.

He watched as she lifted one leg out the window, followed by the other, and then she was gone.

"Did you have a good rest?" Joy asked, good-naturedly, when Clinted showed up to relieve her. "I thought maybe you forgot me."

"How could I forget you?" he asked, feeling if anything more tired than when he had gone up to his room—but not sorry.

"Do you want me to circulate?" she asked, switching places with him.

"Take a break, Joy. Don't come down again unless you feel up to it."

She nodded, started away, then turned back and said, "If you have to leave to go to the doc's, call me."

"I will."

She touched his arm and added, "After you close, my door will be unlocked."

He smiled and nodded, and she went upstairs. He hoped she wouldn't take it personally when he closed up and—barring any unforseen circumstances—went right to sleep.

During his shift, Deputy Steve Owen came in for a drink.

"On the house," Clint said, setting a beer in front of the lawman.

"No," Owen said, "I'll pay."

Taking his money Clint asked, "Tell me, Steve. Why is Sideman the sheriff and not you?"

Owen shrugged and said very simply. "I didn't want the job. Even in the Army I was a sergeant, turning down commissions that came my way. I only want to do my job and get paid for it, Clint. I don't want to command. I never have, and I never will." He drank some of his beer and asked, "What does that make me?"

"A man who knows what he wants," Clint answered, "and a very rare breed."

"Sure," Owen said. He finished his beer and dropped a coin on the bar. "Thanks for the beer."

"Is that all you came here for?"

"That, and to warn you. Sideman's getting pressure from Jory and from the mayor about you."

"I could have guessed," Clint said. "I knew that Jory had been to see him."

"The mayor called him in a little while ago," Owen said. "You can be sure he's getting more pressure now. I just thought I'd let you know."

"Thanks, Steve."

The deputy gave a small salute and left the saloon, passing as he did the doctor, who was on his way in.

"I've come for that drink," Doctor Tobin said.

"And my partner?"

"No great change," the young physician answered.

"Who's with him?"

"My nurse, Mrs. Stuart, a very competent woman. Now how about that drink?"

"Whiskey?"

"A beer will do."

Clint served him the beer, then got one for himself.

"Doc, can you make a guess . . . about my partner, I mean?"

The doctor wiped beer foam from his lips with his sleeve and said, "All I can say is that he's not dead yet, and that in itself is a feat. He's tough, Clint. I think he'll make it."

Clint smiled and lifted his mug to the doctor, who

clinked his own against it, and they drank.

With that weight lifted from his mind, Clint Adams could look forward to the following day, when he would start in earnest towards his goal—the one he must reach before leaving the town of Brightwater, and continuing on.

Chapter Thirty-One

During the course of Clint's stay in Brightwater, a few men had become known to him as regulars at the Buckskin Saloon. He pulled aside one of these, an old-timer named Pop Cook, and offered him a job tending bar until Frank Leslie was back on his feet. He would be free to sample the wares, as long as he didn't get falling down drunk on the job. Pop Cook readily agreed, and although Clint would still take a turn behind the bar each day, this did free him for other things.

One of those other things was Miss Jesse Wells.

The following morning Clint checked on Leslie's condition, and Doc Tobin told him that his partner had spent a restful night, and showed signs of gaining strength. He even allowed Clint to speak to him for a few moments.

"Good morning, partner," he greeted the pale, drawn man lying on a bed in the doctor's back room. Mrs. Stuart, a pleasant-looking woman, was close at hand.

"Only a few minutes, now," she warned Clint.

"I know," he told her. He turned back to Leslie and asked, "How are you feeling—or is that a stupid question?"

"Stupid," Leslie said, sounding hoarse. He cleared

his throat, wet his lips and said, "I've had better days."

"I'll bet," Clint said. "Frank, I don't want to take too much time, but I just want to ask you what you remember about the day you got shot."

"Remember," Leslie repeated, thinking. "I remember turning into that side street, and then . . . that's it."

"You didn't even hear the shot?"

He thought a moment, then shook his head slightly and said, "No, I didn't hear a thing."

"No one called out to you, or anything?"

"No," his partner answered, then thought a moment and repeated, "No, nothing."

"That's enough," Mrs. Stuart said; Clint looked at her, and then nodded.

"Take care, Frank," he said, "I'll be back to see you later."

"Bring some food, I'm hungry."

The nurse looked at Clint and shook her head no, but Clint said, "I'll bring something," which earned him a dirty look from her.

As Clint started to leave, Leslie called out, "How are things at the saloon?"

"Fine," Clint answered. "So good, in fact, that I'm thinking about buying you out."

"Get lost," Leslie said, smiling wanly, and Clint waved and left the room.

"He seems to be in good spirits," he told the doctor.

"He should start making some definite progress now that he's out of danger," Tobin said.

"Good. Doctor, would you like me to pay you something now?" he asked, going into his pocket.

The doctor held up his hand and said, "When the patient is well again, I'll bill you."

Clint thanked the man and told him not to worry about having to pay for his drinks at the Buckskin.

"I'll take you up on that," Tobin promised.

Clint shook the man's hand and left the office. His next stop was the bank, but it wasn't to see Sherman Jory. In fact, he hoped to make the stop without running into the bankman at all. The sole purpose of his visit was to invite a young lady to have lunch with him.

"Miss Wells," he said, stopping at her desk.

She looked up, recognized him, and asked, "Do you want to see Mr. Jory?"

"No, I came to see you."

"Me?" she asked, looking puzzled. "Why?"

"I think we should get to know each other a little better," he said, "and I would like to start by taking you to lunch."

"Me?" she asked, adjusting her spectacles on her nose.

"Yes, you. Will you have lunch with me? Please?"

"I—why I, uh, yes, I would like that, Mr. Adams."

"Clint."

"All right . . . Clint."

They set a time for him to come by for her, and again he hoped to be able to do so without running into Jory. If Jory saw that he was showing an interest in the young lady, he could very well use that to his advantage. As it was, it occurred to him that she might already be under orders to accept any invitation from him.

From the bank he went to the sheriff's office to have a quiet discussion with Sideman . . . if that was possible. He seemed to have an excitable effect on the man, and he wanted to rectify that. It would not do to have the sheriff of Brightwater against him.

"What do you want?" Sideman asked as he entered the man's office.

"Nothing," Clint said. "Just to say good morning and ask you if you've found out anything about the shooting."

Sideman examined him for a moment, then sighed and said, "Sit down. Can I get you a cup of coffee?"

"Sure, thanks," Clint said, seating himself.

He accepted the tin cup from Sideman, who then asked, "How's your partner?"

"He's improving. I spoke to him today."

"Do you think I'd be able to talk to him?"

"I guess so, but he'll tell you the same thing he told me."

"Which is?"

"He didn't see or hear anything before he was shot. He doesn't even recall hearing the shot."

"Wonderful," the man said. His shoulders slumped and he said, "I don't mind telling you I'm stumped, Adams. Maybe my inexperience is costing me."

"I wouldn't think so," Clint said. "No one expected you to be a detective when you took this job, just a town sheriff."

"I guess, but it's still frustrating. One of the rooms in the hotel overlooking that street was vacant. Anyone could have gone in there and waited for Leslie to pass."

"Let's kick it around," Clint said. "What would make the shooter think that Leslie would come down that street?"

"It wouldn't make sense to believe that he took up a position at that window each day, waiting for him to pass."

"No, it makes more sense to believe that he followed him and, on that given day, projected that Frank would walk that way. The hotel has a back door, I suppose."

"Yes."

"Then he could have gotten in that way."

"With a key?"

"With or without, one way or another," Clint said, "but since you mentioned a key, let's talk about the room over the general store."

"I already talked to Sam, and he said no one got by him."

"Well, I talked to him, also, and he told me that there is another key to that back door."

"Another key?" Sideman asked, sitting up straight. "Why the hell didn't he tell me that?"

"He's got a silent partner who wants to stay silent," Clint said.

"Who?"

"He wouldn't say, but if you'll permit me, I've got a hunch."

"Who—" Sideman started to ask, but then he stopped and squinted suspiciously at the Gunsmith. "You aren't going to tell me—"

"Sherman Jory."

"You think Jory bought into the business at some time or another—"

"That's a nice way of putting it."

"All right. So he used his position to acquire at least a piece of the business."

"Right, and as part owner, he has keys to all the locks, including the back door."

"You think Jory went through the back door to that room and shot Frank Leslie?"

"If he's involved—and notice I'm still giving him the benefit of the doubt by saying *if*—I doubt that he did the actual shooting."

"Martin Cort?" the sheriff asked.

"Don't you find that an odd pair?"

"To tell the truth, I've always thought that—but that doesn't make Jory the man you claim he is."

"No, it doesn't, but who else in town would own a piece of a business and want to keep it quiet? The mayor?"

"Ellis?" Sideman said in disbelief.

"Ellis and Jory are very close, aren't they?"

"Like—" Sideman started, but stopped himself short.

"You were going to say 'like thieves,' weren't you?" Clint asked the lawman.

"As a matter of fact, I was," Sideman said. "More coffee?"

"No, thanks."

"All right, Adams, I'm going to ask," the sheriff said, as if he'd just made the decision. "What would you do next?"

"I'd try and find out for sure who the silent partner is in that general store, then try and find out where he was at the time of the shooting, and where that key was."

"He's going to want to know how I know he has a partner," Sideman said.

"Question Jackson again, try and get him to tell you about it," Clint said, rising. "If he doesn't, then go ahead and tell him that I spilled the beans. From there you can try to get him to admit who it is. Maybe he'll even know if Jory—if it is Jory—owns any other businesses in town."

"What are you going to be doing?"

"Me?" Clint asked, heading for the door. "I've got a lunch date with a lovely young lady."

"You're really going to leave Jory alone, as I ask?" Sideman said, although Clint didn't exactly remember being "asked."

Clint shrugged and said, "You're the sheriff, Sheriff. What you say goes."

"Why do I feel like I'm being diddled?" Sideman said. "Get out of here, Adams . . . and thanks."

Chapter Thirty-Two

Clint met Jesse Wells at the bank at the agreed time, and they got away without having to face Sherman Jory. He took her to the same café where they had first met and asked for a corner table.

"I want you all to myself," he told her, and to himself added, *and my back to the wall.*

After they had ordered Jesse asked, "Would you like to tell me now why you asked me to lunch?"

"Do you need more of a reason than I gave you this morning?" he asked.

"You do," she said.

"And what do you think my real reason is?"

She blushed and lowered her eyes, then became bold and said, "I think that maybe you want me to help you."

"To do what?"

"To get the better of Mr. Jory."

"Why would you do that?"

"I wouldn't."

"Well, then, let's have lunch and forget it," he suggested.

She frowned and said, "What do you mean, forget it?"

"Just what I said. We'll have a nice lunch, and then you'll go back to work."

"I don't understand."

"Did you think I would try to force you to help me?"

"I don't know what I expected," she admitted. "You're a puzzling man. You don't seem like—"

"Like what?" he asked when she stopped herself. "Like a gunman, a killer? Is that what Jory told you?"

"No, he didn't—well, yes, he said something—"

"And I don't fit the part, do I?"

"No," she said sternly. "You don't."

The waitress came with their lunches, and they remained silent until she had set them down and gone.

"What kind of man—" Jesse started to ask, but Clint waved her off and said, "Let's eat lunch. You have to be back at work soon, don't you?"

"Yes."

"We'll talk again," he promised. "Maybe over dinner?"

"I don't know," she answered, and he didn't press her.

"We'll talk again, soon," he said, and started eating his lunch.

Afterward, he walked her back to the bank without much conversation passing between them. At one point, while crossing the street, he put a hand to the small of her back and he felt her jump slightly at his touch. Again, when mounting the boardwalk, he took her by the elbow, then allowed his hand to slide to her hip. He thought he felt her lean into his touch, and then moved his hand away.

"I'll call on you again, Jesse, if that's all right with you," he said.

"If you wish."

"I do. Have a good day."

She entered the bank and he started back to the saloon, thinking about her. He was sure that he was dealing with a woman who had long been repressing her physical desires. Just in touching her twice he had been able to feel the tension in her body, like a taut bowstring. She needed someone to help her release that tension, and for selfish reasons, he wanted to be that someone.

Chapter Thirty-Three

While Clint was having lunch with Jesse Wells, three strangers rode into town, one man riding in front, and two behind him, abreast of each other.

The man in front was named Holt, but he was better known as "Saber." Had he been born in another century, he would have been a buccaneer or a pirate. He wore a .45 on his right hip, and alongside his left he wore a saber. He was equally adept with either weapon.

Behind him rode Gault and Coe. Both men made their livings with their guns. They were guns for hire; they did not deal in speed, they dealt simply in death.

The three rode to the livery and left their horses to be cared for. When they asked the liveryman where the best place in town to get a drink was, the man directed them to the Brightwater and to Kelly's, "for all their needs."

They walked down the street the same way they had ridden into town, with the big man in front and the other two behind him. That was the way they entered Kelly's.

The first floor of Kelly's was massive. One entire side of the room was taken up by the bar, and there were tables set up for every type of gambling you could want. To the right there were over-stuffed chairs and divans, on which sat Kelly's girls, of which you could

125

have your pick, for the right price. Pick your girl, and then she took you upstairs, where there were over a dozen rooms available. In a bigger town, Kelly's would have been a gold mine.

In Brightwater the owners were very well off.

Katie Kelly, a bosomy, middle-aged woman who had served her time as a whore and now owned—or half-owned, with banker Jory, anyway—Kelly's, saw the men enter and felt a tingle in her groin that she hadn't felt for years. The big one in front was the reason. He was massive, well over six feet and wide in the shoulders. He had a face that was so ugly it was irresistible.

Kate had a figure that now, at best, could be called blowsy, but she still wore low-cut dresses to show off her breasts. She approached the big man now and hoped he was taking a good look. Maybe he liked experienced women.

"Hello, stranger," she greeted him. "Can I help you?"

He stared at her with cold, slate gray eyes that chilled her and excited her, and said, "My associates and I need some whiskey, some food, and some relaxation."

"You've come to the right place, then," she assured him. "Which would you like first?"

"The whiskey."

"Well, belly up to the bar, then. We have the best whiskey in the state. After that, there's a dining room in the back, or you can eat upstairs, with one of the girls."

She inclined her head towards the other side of the room, where the girls were seated, waiting to be called upon.

She deliberately brushed her full breasts against the

man's arm and said, "I'd say you could just about have your pick, friend."

He moved his arm away from the contact and led the way to the bar. She felt compelled to follow and stood next to him while he ordered his drink.

She watched him down the whiskey, enjoying the way his throat moved when he swallowed. No man had affected her this way before, and it was a new experience for her. She was forty-four and had spent thirty-two years in this business. She doubted that this big man would pick her over some of the younger girls, and cursed the luck that had caused her to finally find a man who could probably make her body sing, but too late for it to do her any good.

He ordered another whiskey, downed that one, then turned to his associates and said, "You're on your own, boys. I'll meet you at the nearest hotel." He did not have to tell them to get their own room, because that was the drill. Saber in one room, Gault and Coe in another.

Coe headed for the dining room, because of all the pleasures in life, for him food was the greatest. He was blessed with the ability to eat all he wanted without adding poundage to his rail thin form.

Gault, on the other hand, had a satyrlike appetite when it came to sex, and he quickly picked out two of the youngest girls to take upstairs—for a start.

Katie watched the two men split up, then looked back at their leader and asked, "What's your pleasure? Food or sex?"

He stared at her with those cold eyes again, and then asked, "Do you work, or just supervise?"

Her stomach fluttered as she answered, "Mister, with you it wouldn't be work."

He examined her for a long moment while she

chewed her lips and held her breath, and then said, "You'll do," and the butterflies that were in her stomach jumped up between her ample breasts.

"Mister, you won't be sorry," she told him, taking hold of his muscular right arm and crushing it against her ample breasts. Her nipples were already hard, and her pussy was hot. God, but she was ready.

As it turned out, however, she wasn't quite ready for what Saber had in mind.

Chapter Thirty-Four

"Miss Wells," Sherman Jory called from his office door.

Jesse Wells looked up from her desk. It was odd for Mr. Jory to summon her with only five minutes left before closing.

"Sir?"

"Would you come into my office, please?"

"Yes, sir."

She entered his office and he said, "Close the door, please, and take a seat."

She did as he asked and then looked at him expectantly. Jory shuffled some papers on his desk, making the girl wait until he was good and ready. It was only when she began to fidget around in her seat that he looked up and spoke.

"I understand that you had lunch with Clint Adams, today."

"Uh, yes, sir, I did," she replied, frowning.

"Are you aware that he is a client of this bank?"

"Yes, sir."

"I don't like my employees socializing with bank clients, Miss Wells. I don't know if you are aware of that."

"It has never been specifically mentioned to me, sir," she said.

"Well, I'm mentioning it now," he pointed out.

"Normally, I do not approve."

The emphasis that her employer put on the word *normally* did not escape Jesse Wells.

"What do you mean?" she asked.

"I mean that in this case, I approve."

"I don't understand."

He leaned forward and clasped his hands on the desk top.

"Miss Wells, I believe that you are a loyal employee of this bank. Am I wrong?"

"Yes, sir—I mean, no, sir. I like to think I'm very loyal."

"If that's the case, then you'll continue to see Mr. Clint Adams . . . if he so desires, of course."

"Why?"

"Because he and his partner owe this bank a lot of money. I would like to know what is going on with them, and the Buckskin Saloon. I have someone on the inside, but I can use all the help I can get."

"What do you want me to do?"

"Oh, talk to him, listen to him . . . maybe get close to him, if you understand my meaning."

She did, and she averted her eyes, hoping that she wasn't blushing.

"I don't know if I can do that."

"Of course you can," he said. "You're a lovely young girl, Miss Wells." He stood up, walked around the desk and approached her. Standing next to her he put his fingertips beneath her chin and tilted her head up. "A very lovely young girl," he added, running his fingers along her jawline.

"Please," she said, pulling her face away.

"Do you need this job?"

"Yes," she said in a whisper.

"In that case, I would think our conversation over,"

he said. He walked quickly back behind his desk and said, "That's all for now, Miss Wells. I have to close up."

"Yes, sir," she said. She got shakily to her feet and walked out of the office. Sherman Jory's eyes—the way he looked at her—had always made her nervous, but he had never before touched her.

Men had touched her before, and she had felt nothing. Sherman Jory touched her, and she felt ill. Then she thought back to that afternoon, when Clint Adams had touched her, ever so slightly, on two occasions. She had felt very different, then, very different indeed.

Jory followed her to the front door of the bank, and she could feel his eyes on her.

"Good night, Miss Wells."

"Good night, Mr. Jory," she replied.

She stepped out and he locked the doors behind her without any further conversation.

"Hi," Clint Adams said, stepping out of the next doorway.

"Oh!"

"Did I frighten you?" he asked.

"Not really," she said. "You simply startled me."

"I didn't want Jory to see me," he explained.

"Why not?"

"He's not one of my favorite people."

"I see."

"He's not one of your favorites either, is he?" Clint asked.

"What makes you say that?"

"The look on your face when you said good night to him."

"He's my boss," she said, as if that explained a lot.

"That doesn't mean a thing."

"I would like to believe that."

He moved closer to her, and she held her breath.

"Let's have dinner, and talk about it," he suggested, taking her hands.

She closed her eyes and became aware of his breath hitting her face, and said, "All right, Clint."

Chapter Thirty-Five

A half hour after dark Martin Cort entered the Brightwater hotel—the nearest hotel to Kelly's—and met the man called Saber in the lobby.

"What about the others?"

Saber pinned Cort's ears back with his slate gray stare and said, "Let's go."

Cort shrugged and led the way. When Saber realized where Cort was taking him he growled, "The back way?"

"Mr. Jory doesn't want anyone to know he's seen you," Cort explained.

"As long as he pays enough."

They continued on in silence and, at the back door to the bank, Cort produced a key.

"You a banker?" Saber asked.

"Hell, no," Cort said. "I'm like you."

"What?"

The one word came out so cold that Cort hunched his shoulders and turned to look at the big man.

"I said, I'm like you. I—I handle a gun."

"Is that so?" Saber asked, looking Cort up and down.

"Sure," Cort said. "I'm Mr. Jory's top gun."

"No wonder he needs me. Let's go. I don't have all night."

Cort debated arguing with the big man, then backed

off and convinced himself it wasn't from fear. After all, Jory was his employer, and he *was* waiting to see the man.

"Okay," Cort said. He opened the door and they went in. When they reached the door to Jory's office it was closed, and Cort knocked.

"Come in, Cort."

To Saber the voice sounded annoyed and superior. Without even seeing Sherman Jory, he decided that he wasn't going to like the man, but luckily he didn't have to like him to take his money.

When Cort opened the door, Saber brushed past him, knocking him back with very little effort.

"Are you Jory?"

Sherman Jory looked up at the massive man facing his desk and felt fear, immediate fear. He was annoyed with himself for this, but there was no way he could have helped it. The ugly face, the wide shoulders, the way the man stood, with one hand on his gun and the other resting on the pommel of a saber. A saber, for Christ's sake!

"I'm Jory," the banker answered.

"I'm Saber."

"Yes. Would you like to take a seat?"

"I'll stand," Saber said. "I'd appreciate it if we got right to the point."

"A drink?"

"No."

Jory looked past Saber to Martin Cort, whose idea it was to call for this man. If Jory was going to use him, he was going to have to establish control, as he had done in the beginning of his relationship with Cort.

Only this man was not Martin Cort.

"I think I'll have a drink," Jory said. "Martin, would you pour, please?"

"Stop right there, Cort!" Saber said, without looking at Cort.

"I beg your—" Jory started, but Saber didn't give him a chance to finish.

"Look, Jory, I didn't come here to drink with you, or to play games. You got a job you want me to do, tell me about it, otherwise I've wasted my time."

"Mr. Jory," Cort said, "you don't need him. I told you that. I can handle Frank Leslie and Clint Adams."

"Calling him was your idea," Jory said.

"No, sir," Cort replied. "Calling someone in was your idea, I simply recommended—"

"Enough!"

The command was so powerful that both bickering men fell silent and stared at the man called Saber.

Turning to Martin Cort, Saber said, "Son, I get the impression that you don't think I'm needed here in Brightwater. That the case?"

"Uh, yeah, that's the case," Cort replied, hitching up his gunbelt.

Turning to Jory, Saber asked, "Are we talking about going up against Buckskin Frank Leslie and the Gunsmith?

"They're involved, yes," Jory said. "Whether or not you'll have to go up against them is going to be up to them."

"And you think you can outdraw Buckskin Frank Leslie?" the man asked Cort.

"And Clint Adams," Cort said boldly.

"We won't even talk about him," Saber said. "You're shooting too high as it is."

"What's that mean?" Cort demanded, his right hand hovering over his six-gun.

"It means if you go for that gun now, you'll lose your hand," Saber said.

"You think you can shoot it off?" Cort asked, beads of sweat forming on his brow.

"I wouldn't have to shoot it off," Saber said. "I'd lop it off."

"With that?"

"With this," Saber said, touching the pommel of his saber again.

"You can draw that saber faster than a man can draw a six-gun?" Jory asked.

"Faster then he can, anyway," Saber said, indicating Martin Cort.

"That can't be."

"If I can," Saber said, "will you shut up and let me and your boss finish our business?"

"Mister, I'd shut up forever."

"Don't be rash, Cort," Jory warned.

"No, I been telling you for a long time I'm all you need," Cort said to his boss, "now I'm gonna prove it."

Saber turned to face Cort full on and said, "Anytime you feel lucky."

"What do you mean?" Cort asked, looking puzzled. "You want me to draw on you?"

"That's right," Saber said, "and you'd better mean it, because I do."

"Now, wait a minute," Jory protested. "This is my office—"

"Quiet," Saber said, and it was just as effective as his previous command.

"Look, Saber—" Cort began, all of a sudden thinking that maybe this wasn't such a good idea. He had expected some kind of contest, not a man-to-man confrontation. He didn't figure on risking his life just to prove a point.

"Come on, son," Saber said, although he wasn't all

that much older than Cort. "Make your move. You don't have a choice anymore."

Jory watched both men. Cort, sweating and chewing his bottom lip while he flexed and unflexed his hand, and Saber, who was plainly relaxed and unworried.

The banker saw Cort go for his gun, saw him clear leather with it, but all he saw of the saber was a flash of silver, and then Cort's gun was flying across the room.

The look on Cort's face was one of pure fright as he frantically examined his right hand to see if it was still there.

It was.

Saber had cleanly knocked the gun out of his hand without injuring him.

"Jesus," he whispered. He watched as Saber restored the blade to its scabbard.

"I left you your hand, son, as a reminder. Don't overestimate its ability."

Cort was at a loss for words, Jory noticed. Either that or he remembered what he said about never talking again if he lost.

"Pick up your gun," Saber told him, and that was the last time he spoke to Cort that night. "I think you and I have some business to discuss," he said to Jory.

"The fact that you're dealing with Buckskin Frank Leslie and the Gunsmith doesn't change your mind?" the banker asked.

"No," Saber said, "it doesn't change my mind. It makes it up." Saber lowered his powerful frame into a chair and said, "Let's talk money."

Chapter Thirty-Six

During dinner Jesse Wells thought about what Sherman Jory had said to her, and also about the way she felt, being with Clint Adams. After dinner she discovered that she wanted to either go back to his room with him, or take him to hers, and she wanted it for herself, not because of any loyalty to the bank, or to Jory. In fact, she didn't even want to go back to the bank anymore.

"Jesse—"

"Yes," she said, firmly.

"You don't even know what I was going to ask you," Clint said, laughing.

"The answer is yes, Clint, and if I'm wrong about the question then I'm just making a fool out of myself." She reached across the table to touch his hand and asked, "Am I wrong?"

"No, Jesse, you're not wrong."

"Should we go to your room?"

"No," he said. "My room is over the saloon, and that's no place for a lady like you."

"My room, then."

"People might talk—"

"I don't care," she said, standing up. Her breath was already coming faster as she said, "I don't care about much anymore."

He stood up and said, "Let's go, then."

They walked to Jesse's room, which was above the general store.

"You live here?" he asked, surprised.

"Yes. Mr. Jackson rents me a room."

"The one off the side street?"

She frowned at him and said, "No, the one across from it."

"You have a key to the back door?"

"No, just to the front. Why?"

"No reason," he told her. "No reason at all."

It was after closing for the store, but she let them in with her key and led the way up the same stairs he had taken to go up and see that other room.

"Does Mr. Jackson also live here?"

"No, he has a house at the south end of town. The other room is vacant."

When they got to her room she put down her bag and turned to face him.

"I'm frightened," she confessed.

"Why?"

"Because I've never felt like this," she said. Her heart was beating so loud that she was sure he could hear it. "My legs are weak."

"Maybe you need someone to help you stand," he suggested. He walked up to her and put his hands on her waist. Again he was aware of how tightly strung she was. "I want to help you relax," he said.

"Oh God," she breathed, and fell against him with her hand on his chest.

"What is it?"

"I want to tell you something before we—we start," she whispered.

"What?"

"Mr. Jory called me in today, just before we closed."

He waited a moment, then said, ''Yes?''

''He wanted me to—to continue to see you. He said I should be—be nice to you, if that was what it took. Do you know what I mean?''

''Yes,'' he said. He grinned, but she couldn't see it. ''I know what you mean.''

She looked up at him and said, ''This has nothing to do with that. Do you believe me?''

He smiled at her, released her waist and removed her glasses.

''Yes, I believe you.''

He bent to kiss her and her lips trembled beneath him. She was tentative at first, then bolder, but her passion was still held at bay beneath the surface. He knew that it would either come right out, or he'd have to work it out, but when it did come it was going to be as if a dam had burst.

When it happened, that would be his reward for his efforts.

But first, there was something he wanted to tell her . . .

''Jesse,'' he said, his lips only inches from hers. ''There's something I have to tell you.''

''I know,'' she said. ''You wanted to use me against Mr. Jory, just as he wanted to use me against you.''

''Yes, but—''

She placed her fingers over his lips and said, ''You don't have to say anything. I don't care. I don't care . . .'' she said, and she pressed her lips to his again. He probed tentatively with his tongue, easing her mouth open, and then thrusting his tongue inside.

''God . . .'' she whispered, and backed away from him. She started to undress, and he felt her embarrassment, so he did not watch her, much as he would have liked to. Instead, he began undressing himself. He did so without hesitation, so that he was finished much sooner than she was. Naked, he turned to look at her and she was clad only in her camisole; he could see the goose bumps that had been raised on her arms.

"Cold?" he asked.

"No," she said, smiling wanly. "Still frightened."

"There's nothing to be frightened of," he assured her.

As she finished undressing she could not take her eyes off his erection. She was not a virgin, but she had not had many men, and he was easily the biggest.

When she was naked he admired her breasts. The dusky nipples were beginning to blossom, and he saw that her breasts were fuller than they appeared while she was dressed. Not as full as Joy Darlings's, or Marlene Jory's, but full and lovely just the same.

"You're beautiful," he said, and she blushed and averted her eyes. "There's still something else, though."

"What?" she asked, looking at him.

"Your hair."

"Oh," she said.

She reached up to unpin her hair, and he enjoyed the way her breasts rose and pointed themselves at him. Her hair fell down to her shoulders and he said, "Now you're incredible," and she blushed again.

He moved to her and immediately took her breasts in his hands. They were smooth and firm. He gathered her into his arms and pulled her against him. She felt his erection trapped between them and marveled at how hot the column of flesh was.

"Warm?" he asked.

"Hmm," she said, closing her eyes. She was trying to give herself up to the sensations, trying to release the control she normally had on her emotions.

He let her go and pulled the covers down on the bed. Awkwardly she got in first, and then he followed.

"This is very natural, Jesse," he said. "I've thought about it since the first time we met."

"Oh, so have I," she replied.

He kissed her mouth, then lowered his head and kissed each of her breasts. She shivered, but not from the cold. As he rolled one nipple between his lips, and then his teeth, she moaned aloud and grasped his head. He sucked on her nipples until she couldn't take anymore.

"Please," she said, her hips twitching uncontrollably, "please, now. I can't wait."

"Yes," he said, and when he drove himself into her, he felt the dam burst. She heaved up beneath him, and it was all he could do to stay with her. He hadn't thought it would take this short a time, but she was letting herself go.

She herself was amazed at how simple it had been. When he had entered her it was the easiest thing in the world—and the rightest thing—just to give herself up to him. She felt his hands cup her buttocks and lift her to him, steadying her, and then he was taking her in long, deep strokes, and she wasn't cold anymore.

She would never be cold again.

Chapter Thirty-Seven

Joy saw the man with the saber enter the saloon, followed closely by two other men who, by comparison, were unremarkable. The big man approached the bar, and the other two followed, and they all ordered drinks from Pop, who was having the time of his life tending bar.

Joy decided that maybe it was time for her to change her mind about selling herself. The big man looked like he'd have the price.

She went up to the bar and said, "Hello."

The big man was in the act of bringing his drink to his mouth and he did not allow her to stop him. He downed the whiskey, and then looked at her.

"Hello."

"Can we get you anything else, besides a drink?"

"I don't think so," he said. She looked disappointed and he added, "Maybe one of my friends—"

"I don't think so," she said, mimicking him.

"What's the matter?" he asked, turning to face her. "My friends aren't good enough for you?"

She placed her hands on her hips and responded to him boldly. "It was an exclusive offer."

"You think you're exclusive, huh?" he asked her. "Just because you've got big tits."

"Hey—" she began to protest, but he reached out with one massive hand, grabbed her right breast and twisted it. The pain was bad, but she didn't scream. "Christ," she said, grabbing his wrist.

"Hey, you—" Pop yelled, reaching under the bar for an axe handle that was always there. But before he could grab it, one of the other men struck him across the face with his six-gun, knocking him down.

"What's going on?" Joy cried out, still trying to break the grip the big man had on her.

"Come on, sweetheart," he said, grabbing her other breast now. "Isn't this what you had in mind for us?"

"Stop it! Why are you doing this?"

"You insulted my friends," he said, "and they want to leave you something to remember them by. Coe," he said, and passed her along to one of his friends.

The others in the saloon had been watching up to that point, and now a couple of men stood up and moved towards the bar.

"Take her in the back," Saber told Coe.

"Sure."

"And don't take too long," Gault called after him, anxious to sample those breasts himself.

"Let her go," one of the customers said.

Coe hesitated, but Saber said, "Go ahead." He turned to face the two men, with his back to the bar, and for the first time his saber came into view.

The other man put his hand on the arm of the man who had spoken and said, "That's Saber."

"I can see his saber," the first man said, "but I'd be more worried about his gun."

"No, you don't understand—" the second man said, but the first man moved away from him and towards Saber.

"I said let her go, mister."

"Make me."

The first man went for his gun and his friend

shouted, "No!" but too late. The saber flashed and imbedded itself in the first man's belly, and he hadn't even gotten his gun out. With a stunned look on his face, he clutched at his belly and fell to the floor.

"Coe," Saber called.

"Yeah?" Coe answered. He had just reached the door to the back room.

"Let her go," Saber ordered, and Coe released Joy. At the same time, Pop staggered up from the floor, leaning on the bar, blood streaming from a cut on his forehead.

"All right, boys," Saber said, cleaning the blood from his Saber with the dead man's clothes, "bust the place up."

As Gault and Coe pulled their guns, the place emptied out, fast. Joy watched from the back of the room as the two men fired at anything that was breakable—windows, glasses, bottles—littering the place with shattered glass.

"No," Pop said again, reaching for the ax handle. Saber turned and nonchalantly drove his blade into Pop's chest.

"No!" Joy screamed.

Saber put his blade away and crossed the room in a few quick, long strides to face Joy.

"No," she whispered.

The firing had stopped, and Coe and Gault were reloading.

"Saber," Coe called out, "the law should be here, soon."

"The law here is a schoolteacher," Saber said over his shoulder, "but don't worry, we'll be gone in a second." He looked at Joy and said, "Make sure you give my compliments to the Gunsmith. My name is Saber. Can you remember that?"

When she didn't answer he slapped her across the face.

"Can you remember that, bitch?"

"Yes," she said, hoarsely, holding her hand to her cheek.

"Say it! Say my name."

"Saber."

"That's a good whore," he said, and then his left hand came across so that the back of it struck her left cheek. The skin over her cheekbone split open, and she fell to the floor, unconscious.

"Anything else?" Coe asked Saber.

"Just take care of the stock behind the bar, and let's get going," the big man said. "No sense tangling with that schoolteacher-sheriff if we don't have to."

"Right," Coe said. He and Gault faced the bar and opened fire, shattering as many bottles as they could without reloading.

"All right!" Saber called out. "Take a few bottles for our trouble and let's get going."

Gault went around behind the bar, found two bottles of whiskey that were still in one piece and tossed one to Coe. As he came back around the bar he stopped to look at the fallen Joy, admiring her breasts.

"Big, ain't they?"

"Come on," Saber said. "There are plenty of tits around."

"We staying in town?"

"No. Jory has arranged for a place."

"Then just let me get one feel, for the road."

"Gault," Saber said, "women will be the death of you, yet."

"If I have my choice," Gault said, grinning.

At the time of the shooting, Clint Adams was bringing Jesse Wells to the brink of another climax. He did not hear the shots; all he heard were her cries for more, and he did his best to give it to her.

When Sheriff Tom Sideman arrived at the Buckskin Saloon, Saber and his men were gone. All Sideman found were two dead men, an unconscious woman, and a saloon that was in a shambles.

He had not responded to the shooting immediately, because he had been at Kelly's. It seemed that someone had gone up to the second floor with Katie Kelly herself, and had beaten the whorehouse madame half to death.

The description he had gotten of the man she had gone upstairs with was complete, right down to the fact that the man was wearing a saber, as well as a six-gun.

When he saw how the bartender and the other dead man in the saloon had been killed, he thought that it was too much of a coincidence. Joy Darling had been taken to the doctor's office, and when she was able to talk, he'd find out what the story was. In the meantime he'd try to locate any customers that had been in the saloon at the time.

He also wondered where Clint Adams was, and what he had been doing at the time his saloon had been getting torn apart.

He hoped that whatever it was, it had been worth the price.

Chapter Thirty-Eight

By the time Clint left Jesse Wells's bed, he had realized that he couldn't use her against her boss. Using Marlene Jory against him, however, was another matter entirely. She was quite willing to help Clint, and as of now he was quite willing to accept.

As he approached the Buckskin Saloon, he saw the crowd out front, and his heart sank.

"Excuse me," he said, elbowing his way through. When he reached the doors he saw Steve Owen standing just inside. "Steve."

"Clint, where have you been?"

Clint was about to answer when he stepped through the doors and saw the condition of the place. "Jesus Christ, what the hell happened here?"

At the sound of his voice Sheriff Sideman turned. "Where have you been?"

"With a lady," Clint answered. "You mind telling me what happened here?"

"Three men came in and busted up the place."

"Just what I needed," Clint said. He took a few steps into the room and noticed that almost everything that was made of glass had been shattered. Then he noticed the blood on the floor. "They busted up more than just my place," he said, turning to look at Sideman. "What happened?"

"They killed two men," Sideman said. "A customer and your bartender."

"Pop Cook?" Clint asked. "God, he just started—it was only supposed to be part-time, until my partner got back on his feet." He covered the bottom portion of his face with his hand, then looked at Sideman and asked, "What about Joy? Where is she?"

"She's at the doc's," Sideman said. "She got beaten up pretty good."

"By who?"

"That's what I want to find out," Sideman said. "There were a bunch of customers in here, but nobody has come forward yet."

"Who was the dead man?"

"Local ranch hand."

Clint looked around further, his anger growing, and then he turned to Sideman and said, "Jory—"

"Don't start jumping to any conclusions," Sideman broke in. "I'll talk to Jory and find out about his whereabouts tonight—"

"His whereabouts don't matter," Clint insisted. "He hired this out—"

"Clint—" Sideman started, then stopped short in frustration. "I'm going over to Doc Tobin's to talk to your girl. Do you want to come along?"

"Definitely."

"All right. Close up, I'll wait for you."

While Clint was closing up, Sideman gave Owen orders to try and find out who the dead man had been with—if anyone.

As he and Clint walked to the doctor's office, Clint asked, "Is Steve the only deputy you have?"

"I have a couple of men I could call on, but there's never been the need," the lawman explained, and then he added, "But if you and Leslie stick around here a little longer, I may have to."

"We're not looking for trouble, Sheriff."

"I understand that, Clint, but you have to admit that men like you and Leslie just naturally attract it. I don't want anyone in town getting caught in a crossfire, like tonight."

"How were the hand and Pop killed?"

"They were stabbed."

"Stabbed? While a saloon full of people watched? Did you find a knife?"

"We didn't find anything. I'm hoping your girl, Joy, will be able to talk—"

"Why wouldn't she be?"

"Her face was all swollen up, Clint. I'm no doctor, so let's wait and see what's what, okay?"

When they got to Tobin's office the doctor had just finished examining Joy Darling.

"How is she, Doc?" Clint asked.

"Her cheekbone may be broken," he said, "I can't be sure. In any case, she's got a nasty cut and a bad bruise."

"Can she talk?" Sideman asked.

"I was just about to give her something to make her sleep. She's in pain."

"I'd like a chance to talk to her first," the lawman said.

"All right, but not for too long."

Clint started to follow the sheriff, but Tobin put his hand on his chest and said, "Not both of you."

"I'll let you know what she says," Sideman promised, and went into the examining room.

"How's my partner?"

"He's awake and wants to know what's going on," Tobin said. "I think that in the morning you'll be able to move him to his room.''

"Have you seen the two dead men?''

"Briefly.''

"They were knifed?''

"They were stabbed,'' Tobin said, ''but I doubt a knife was used. The wounds are too deep. It's more likely that some kind of a sword was used.''

Clint went cold and asked, ''Like a saber?''

"Exactly.''

And there were three men, Clint reminded himself. "Can I talk to my partner?''

"Sure. Go ahead. I'll check in on my other patient.''

Clint went into the back room, where Leslie immediately asked, ''What the hell is going on? Was that Joy they brought in?''

"Yes,'' Clint said, pulling a chair over and sitting down by Leslie's bed. ''Seems like three men went into the Buckskin tonight, killed Pop Cook and another man, beat up Joy and broke the place up.''

"Christ, who were they?''

"Sideman is trying to find that out now, from Joy, but I think I've got an idea.''

"Who do you think it was? Jory?''

"Oh, I don't have any doubt but that he hired it done,'' Clint said. He told Leslie how the men were killed. ''A saber, Frank. That mean anything to you? Three men, one wearing a saber and a side-arm?''

"Can't say that it does.''

"You'd've had to spend some time up North to have heard about him,'' Clint said. ''A man named Holt, better known as Saber.''

"Saber,'' Leslie said, turning the name over on his tongue. ''Seems to me I might have heard tell of a man called that. Is his gun for sale?''

"His gun and his blade."

"And now he's here."

"Yeah. It looks like Jory might be getting serious about this."

"Well," Leslie said, starting to sit up, "I guess it's time for this old hoss to get back on his feet."

"Whoa, hoss," Clint said, putting his hand on his partner's chest and gently pushing him back down. "Not just yet."

"You can't figure on facing this Saber alone, not if he's got two men with him."

"They're just back-up," Clint said. "They do a lot of the dirty work—like shooting up our saloon."

"Saber does the killing?"

Clint nodded and said, "Saber does the killing."

"Then you're going to need help," Leslie said, starting to sit up again.

"The doctor says I can take you back to your room in the morning, but you're going to have to stay there. You've got to heal up before you'll do me any good."

"Well, as long as you don't do nothing stupid until I do," Frank Leslie said, "then we've got a deal."

"All right," Clint said, standing up. "You get some sleep and I'll be by in the morning."

"How's Joy?"

"She got beat up some, may have a broken cheek-bone, but she's a lot luckier than Pop Cook and some poor ranch hand."

"Why'd they pick on poor old Pop? I wonder."

"My fault. I gave him a job tending bar until you got back on your feet."

"You can't take the blame for that," Leslie said.

"Sure I can," Clint answered. "I hired him."

"Then I have to take part blame. If I hadn't got shot, you wouldn't have had to hire him."

"That's silly."

"So's your reasoning, so let's not either one of us start blaming ourselves—or each other."

Clint stared down at his partner, then said, "You're pretty smart for a fella who don't have enough sense to get out of the way of a bullet."

"Don't forget it."

"I won't," Clint said. "See you in the morning."

He found the sheriff waiting to see him in the outer office.

"What did she say?"

"She said there were three men, but the one who hit her was a big man wearing a long sword—said he called himself Saber, made a real thing of telling her that. You know him?"

"I know of him," Clint said. "His real name's Elisha Holt, and he's for hire. The other two change, as I understand it. He only uses them for back-up and dirty work."

"I guess he saves beating up women and killing for himself. He beat up Katie Kelly tonight," Sideman explained. "That's where I was when your place was being shot up."

Tobin came out of the room where he'd put Katie Kelly; he looked haggard. "Sure hope you fellas get the scum that did this."

"I do, too," said Sideman. "Oh, Clint—Joy wants to talk to you before the medication takes hold."

"I won't let her talk long," the Gunsmith promised Tobin, and went in to see her.

"Joy," he said, approaching the cot she was lying on. There was a cut and a livid bruise on her left cheek, and her lips were swollen.

"You're going to be fine," he assured her, taking her hand.

"He hurt me," she said.

"I know," he said. "I'll find him."

"He's big . . . dangerous . . ."

"Shhh, I know, Joy. I know who it is."

"There's something else you have to know," she said, her words distorted by her swollen lips, and by the pain she was feeling.

"Tell me tomorrow, Joy," he said.

"Clint—"

He touched his lips to her forehead and whispered again, "Tell me tomorrow. You do what the doctor tells you to do, and I'll see you in the morning."

"Clint—"

"Enough," he told her. "Be a good girl or you're fired."

She might have tried to smile, but she ended groaning from the pain.

He went out and when he noticed that the sheriff was gone, he asked the doctor, "Where'd Sideman go?"

"He went looking for the men who caused all the ruckus."

"He won't find them," Clint said, "not in town, anyway."

"And you will?"

He regarded the doctor for a moment, then shook his head and said, "I won't find him, Doctor. He'll find me."

Chapter Thirty-Nine

When Clint returned to the saloon there was someone waiting for him out front, in the shadows. Marlene Jory.

"Can I come inside?" she asked.

"If you want to help me clean up," he said. "I can't afford to keep this place closed tomorrow. I've got too much invested in it."

"I'll help."

They went inside and while Clint cleaned up behind the bar and restocked it, Marley swept the rest of the saloon. Afterward, Clint made a pot of coffee and they doused all the lamps but one and drank it at a corner table.

"Why'd you come tonight?"

"To warn you," she said, wryly. "Guess I was too late."

"You knew about this?"

"Not soon enough," she said. "I heard my father talking to Cort about it. Something about a man they called Saber, a killer."

"Yes. He killed two people tonight."

"I'm sorry . . . and ashamed."

Clint peered at her in the dim light and saw a girl—no, a woman—he hadn't previously seen. She was more than just a flighty girl who thought that sex was a game.

155

"What are you ashamed of?"

"Of my father," she said. "Of the fact that he is my father, of the way he does business. I came here tonight to warn you about more than just this," she said, indicating the mess they had just cleaned up. "My father said something about having someone on the inside," she said.

"Yes, I know," he said. "He tried to get Jesse Wells to work on me."

"What happened?"

"She changed her mind."

"Or you changed it for her?"

"Maybe I helped . . . a little. But she's a bright girl."

"I see. And pretty, too, I suppose, if you like them . . ."

"Quiet?"

That wasn't what she was going to say, but she smiled and said, "Yes, quiet."

"I like all kinds of women, Marley," he said. "All shapes and sizes and temperaments."

"I bet you do, too," she said.

"Thanks for coming here tonight," he said. "I needed the help."

"Glad I could offer some," she said. She reached out to touch his hand and said, "I could offer more."

"Under normal circumstances," Clint said, "I'd say yes, but I'm beat, and I'd rather your father didn't wonder where you were tonight."

"You may not believe this," she said, "but I understand."

"Oh, I believe it," he assured her. "I believe there's a lot more to Marley Jory than meets the eye."

He walked her to the front door and she gave him a

chaste kiss on the cheek and said, "Let's keep that little bit of information between you and me, okay?"

"Be careful," he told her. "The man your father hired likes to beat up women."

She poked him in the ribs and said, "Hmm, I like your methods much better.

Chapter Forty

The next morning Clint helped Frank Leslie up to his room, and then he took Joy Darling and put her up in his own room.

"I want to be able to keep an eye on both of you easily."

"Well, well," she said through swollen lips, "I had to take a beating to get back into this room with you."

"Joy—"

She held her hand up to him and said, "That's okay, Clint. I'm not a kid anymore, I know the way the world works."

"Joy, I'm sorry if—"

"Don't apologize," she said. "Too many men have apologized and not meant it. I don't want to have to start wondering about you, too."

He started for the door, because she didn't seem to be in the mood for company.

"Oh," he said as he reached it, "there was something you wanted to tell me last night."

"Was there?"

"You seemed to think it was pretty important."

She shook her head and said, "I can't for the life of me think of what it might be. I'm kind of tired, Clint."

"Sure," he said. "We'll talk later."

He walked down the hall to Frank Leslie's room.

"You still in one piece?" he asked his partner.

Leslie was sitting up in bed, propped up by three pillows.

"I never thought I'd get so tired just walking a couple of blocks," he complained.

"A bullet takes a lot out of you."

"You sound like you've caught a few."

"I've had my share. Do you need anything?"

"My guns."

Clint walked over to a chair by the window, where Leslie's twin Cole Peacemakers were hanging. He picked up the gunbelt and hung it on the bedpost near Leslie's uninjured side, where he could get at it in a hurry if he had to.

"What are your plans for the day?" Leslie asked him.

"Well, since I'm the only employee of the Buckskin left on his feet, I guess I'll have to run it alone. We can't afford to have it closed."

"That would please Mr. Jory much too much," Bucksin Frank Leslie agreed. "You're not gonna go looking for Saber and his boys?"

"I'll tell you what I told the doctor last night," the Gunsmith said. "Saber will find me."

"You mean us, don't you?"

"That's right," Clint agreed. "He'll find us when Jory can't wait anymore."

"And we won't be hard to find, will we?" Leslie asked. "Especially me. Is that why you're going to stay around? To look after me?"

"You don't need looking after," Clint said. "At least, not that way. No, I just don't want to be wandering the streets, presenting my back as a target—the way some people do."

"You don't think Saber—"

"—shot you? No, I don't think he or his men were here yet."

"Martin Cort," Leslie said. "My money's on him."

"We'll find out soon enough, Frank, if we just sit tight for a while. Meanwhile, I'll tend bar, and you get some rest."

"Now that," Leslie said, pointing his finger at Clint, "sounds like my idea of a partnership."

Chapter Forty-One

For the next three days Clint was pretty busy, running the saloon, caring for Joy and Leslie, and trying to repair all of the damage to the saloon.

"Jory didn't succeed in closing us down," he told Leslie one night, "but he cost us a few bucks. We're going to need some brisk business to make our next payment."

"How are the poker games doing?"

"I can't tend bar and deal at the same time," Clint answered, "so the games are off for a while."

And that was costing them money, too. Clint couldn't bring himself to hire somebody else as a bartender, though. He didn't want to be responsible for anyone else getting killed.

At the end of the third day Leslie told him, "I'm pretty sure I can take over the bar, Clint."

"You couldn't stand long enough."

"The bar will be there to hold me up," Leslie reasoned. "Come on, partner, with me behind the bar you can start dealing again, and we can start making money again."

The idea made sense—if Leslie was up to it.

"All right, Frank. We'll try it out tomorrow and see how you hold up."

"All right," Leslie said. "What about Joy? How is she?"

"I don't know," Clint replied honestly. "Her face is still bruised, but the swelling has gone down."

"She still wouldn't want anyone to see her like that," Leslie said, understandingly. "No woman would."

"It's more than that," Clint said. "She's not the same. She's quiet, depressed."

"You think she's got something on her mind?"

"Definitely," Clint replied. "That night, when she got beat up, she had something to tell me in the doctor's office. Made a big thing out of it, but I wouldn't let her talk. Now I wish I had."

"She hasn't brought it up?"

"She claims she can't remember wanting to tell me something, but she's lying."

"A woman scorned, maybe?" Leslie asked.

Clint thought about it for a moment. "I don't think so."

"Well, then, I guess it's just something else we'll have to wait to find out."

"I suppose. I'll bring you up some dinner in a little while, on the way back from the café."

"Sure, no hurry."

"I'll lock the place up tight. If you hear anybody walking around in the next hour or so, it won't be me."

"I'll be careful," Leslie said. "You be the same."

Clint made sure the back door was locked, then went out the front, securing it behind him. The waiting game was starting to get to him. Maybe he should do something to push Jory, but what?

"Clint," he heard a voice call out, and turned to find Steve Owen coming toward him.

"Evening, Steve," he said. "Where you headed?"

"The café, to get the sheriff and me some dinner."

"I'm going there myself."

They walked together and Clint asked, "Has Sideman been looking for Saber and his men?"

"Sure, but without any luck."

"I wouldn't expect him to have any."

"No, and I don't think he really does, either, but it's his job—"

"And he's a great one for doing that."

Owen nodded, then asked, "How's Joy . . . and your partner?"

"Both of them are getting along," Clint said. He felt that Owen was more concerned about Joy, asking about Leslie only out of courtesy. "We're going to put my partner behind the bar tomorrow so I can go back to dealing."

"Is he up to it?"

"We'll find out."

The deputy fell silent and Clint had the feeling that there was something on his mind.

"What is it, Steve?"

"Huh? Oh, is it that obvious?"

"That something's on your mind? Yes."

"I was just wondering, do you think Joy would see me tomorrow if I came by?"

"I don't know. She's still pretty bruised. I don't think she wants anyone to see her like that."

"Yeah, I guess . . ."

"Why don't you give it a try though?" Clint suggested. "Can't hurt to try."

"I guess not."

When they got to the café Steve Owen ordered a couple of meals to go out and waited with Clint at his table until they were ready. When they were he stood up, paid for them, and told Clint to enjoy his dinner.

"Thanks."

When the deputy didn't move to leave, Clint looked

up from his own meal and said, "Steve?"

"Look, I know I've got this star on, but if you should find that maybe you . . . need an extra gun . . . you know?"

Clint smiled and said, "I know, Steve. Thanks for the offer."

"Sure. Good night."

"Good night."

Owen was a good man, and Clint wouldn't mind having his gun on their side, but if things went well, he and Leslie would be able to handle things between then, with no one else getting killed.

No one who counted, anyway.

Chapter Forty-Two

Buckskin Frank Leslie lasted about a half a day behind the bar before Clint had to call off the poker game and help him back up to his room.

"I'll do better tomorrow," Leslie promised, and he did.

The day after that he spent the entire day behind the bar and although he looked rather pale by the time they closed up, it was an encouraging sign.

For some . . .

Once again Martin Cort brought the man called Saber into the bank through the back door for a meeting with Sherman Jory.

"We're getting tired of hanging around, Jory," Saber told the banker.

"You won't have to hang around much longer," Jory promised.

"Why?"

"Breaking up their saloon didn't accomplish much," Jory said. "Leslie is back working, and Adams has started dealing his poker game again."

"I thought killing their bartender might slow down business a little," Saber said.

"You weren't supposed to kill anyone," Jory said, "let alone two people."

"Hey, Mr. Banker," Saber said, leaning over the desk and staring Jory in the eyes, "that's what I do."

"Yes," Jory said, "so I'm finding out."

"If you don't like it, just pay me off and I'll move on."

"No, not yet," Jory told him. "I think that perhaps it's time for you to use your true talent."

"Killing?"

Jory nodded and said, "Killing. That is beginning to look like the only way I'm going to get rid of those two."

"How do you want it done?"

"That's up to you," Jory said, "but I don't want to be connected with it, and I don't want you killing any lawmen. Just Frank Leslie—"

"And Clint Adams," Saber said.

"Yes, Clint Adams, too," Jory said.

"When do you want it done?"

"Soon."

"The sooner the better," Saber said, "I'm ready to move on, anyway."

Saber started to leave the room and Cort followed until Jory called him back.

"Cort, I want to talk to you," Jory said. "Stay."

Saber looked at Cort, shrugged and kept going. He didn't like the guy, anyway, although he had to admit that he'd kept his word. Ever since the day he'd disarmed him with the saber, the guy hadn't said two words without being spoken to first.

"See ya," Saber said, and left.

"What is it?" Cort asked.

"Close the door."

Cort closed the door, then turned to face his employer. "That man is dangerous," Jory said.

"Don't I know it."

"He's too dangerous," Jory added. "You know he practically beat Katie Kelly to death."

"I heard something about that, but I wasn't sure that it was him," Cort said.

"He also beat Joy Darling. He likes to beat women."

"And kill men. So?"

"So, I think we're going to make a hero out of you, Cort," Jory told his man. "Whatever Saber plans for Leslie and Adams, you will be part of—only you'll have additional instructions from me, to be acted upon only after he and his men have killed those two. Do you understand?"

"I understand."

"Are you up to it?"

"I've been telling you all along," Cort said. Remembering how Saber had embarrassed him in front of Jory, he said, "Believe me, I'm up to it."

After Cort left, Sherman Jory sat back in his chair and went over his plans again. This was the first time he had really resorted to any kind of serious physical violence, and now he was going to add murder. It couldn't be helped, though. He wasn't going to balk at murder when he was aiming so high. Frank Leslie was the first businessman who had resisted his efforts to control his business, and Clint Adams's involvement had only made it worse. He had to get both men out of the way, for good.

And then there was Saber, and his men. He couldn't allow it to become known that he had hired them, so they would also have to be eliminated. That was where Cort came in . . .

And after Cort got rid of Saber—and Jory fervently hoped he was capable of it—that would be where Cort went out . . .

Even if Saber's men killed Cort, Saber would be dead, and he was the only one who knew who they were working for, so whether Saber's men killed Cort, or Jory's man did, it didn't matter.

And then, eventually, Jory knew that he himself would have to commit murder, to erase the last link to the whole mess. Then he could get on with his grand plan, which might take him all the way to the governor's mansion.

With a little luck . . .

Chapter Forty-Three

With the swelling gone from her face, and the bruises reduced to a point where they could be covered by makeup, Joy moved out of Clint's room and back to her own, and also came back to work. Her disposition, however, did not change. There was still something very much on her mind, and bothering her.

"What do you think it is?" Frank asked Clint as they watched Joy work the place.

"I have an idea, but I don't like it. Marlene Jory told me that her father had somebody on the inside. I assumed he meant his secretary, since he tried to get hers close to me. Now, I'm not sure."

"Joy? Working for Jory?"

"Frank, who owns Kelly's?"

"I don't know. I always thought Katie did."

"Why couldn't Jory?"

"He could," Leslie conceded.

"Which would mean that Joy worked for him, and now she works for us. I'll have to ask Marlene."

"Clint, if Jory could plant Joy with us, why wouldn't he send his daughter after you, pretending she wanted to help?"

"I don't think he planned that far in advance," Clint said. "I think she surprised him by coming back, and he wasn't prepared for it. I think he really didn't want her to meet me that first day. I think her story's for real, Frank, so I'll ask her to help, like she offered.''

''You think she knows all about her father's business practices?''

''Not all, but some, and what she doesn't know, maybe she can find out about. Frank, I think I'll go calling on Miss Jory while her father is at the bank.''

''Be careful, Clint,'' Leslie warned.

Clint circled Jory's house twice before he was finally satisfied that no one was watching it. Apparently, the man had no idea that he had seen Marlene and saw no reason to put a watch on her.

When she answered the door he said, ''I assume your father is at the bank?''

''Every day,'' she answered, giving him a funny look. ''Is it a safe bet that you aren't here because you missed me and desperately need me?''

''It's a fairly good bet, yes,'' he said.

''Come in, before someone sees you.'' Inside she said, ''Can I get you some coffee?''

''Does your father ever come back here during the day?''

''My father doesn't leave the bank until business hours are over—ever!''

''Then I'll have a cup of coffee.''

''And a piece of homemade apple pie?''

''Who made it?''

''I did, silly.''

''I didn't know you could cook.''

''You still don't,'' she said. ''Not until you've tasted the pie.''

''Then I'll have a piece.''

Clint tasted the pie, found it delicious and told her so.

"You sound surprised."

"No reason why I should be," he said. "Coffee's good, too. Just the way I like it, strong."

"Now that you've had your coffee and pie, you want to tell me why you came here?"

"You said you wanted to help. Do you still want to?"

"Yes."

"Where would your father keep any papers that would be important to him?"

"He has an office upstairs. I guess he'd keep them in there. What are you looking for?"

"Well, for one thing, I'd like to know if your father owns all or any part of Kelly's."

"All," she answered. "I know some of the girls, and they know who owns the place."

"How?"

"Because my father has used them all, at one time or another."

"I see."

"He used whores even when my mother was alive, when he had to pay. Now that he doesn't have to pay, he uses them even more. They know who owns them, Clint."

"Do you know how many other businesses he owns in town?"

"I wouldn't be surprised if he owned half the town by now. My father thinks that owning a town is the key to political success."

"It's been a start for some men," Clint admitted. "Would you know what to look for in his desk?"

"Papers, you mean? To show what he owns? I'd know."

"Would you get them, if I needed them?"

"Yes," she said, without hesitation.

"All right," he said, "then I don't have to go upstairs and look myself."

"You just let me know when you want them, and I'll turn them over to you or the sheriff or anyone you want."

He stood up, preparing to leave, then asked another question that occurred to him.

"What do you know about the mayor?"

"Uncle Wesley?" she asked, laughing shortly. "He does whatever my father tells him to. They're both such fine gentlemen, yet each of them would love to have the other's daughter in bed."

"The mayor has approached you?"

"No, and my father hasn't gone after Lucie, but I know what a man's eyes look like when he's thinking about you. I learned that even before I went East."

She approached him and touched his face with her fingertips.

"You have kind eyes, Clint. I don't understand how my father could call you a killer."

"People have a habit of believing reputations, Marley, and not looking that close at a man's eyes."

"That's why women are so much smarter than men."

He took her fingers from his face and kissed them.

"You're probably right, Marley. You're probably right."

Chapter Forty-Four

That same night, while Clint Adams was sitting with his back to the wall, dealing poker to five willing losers, three men walked into the saloon. He didn't recognize any of their faces, but he recognized the big man in the front from the saber he wore.

Joy moved over next to him, her hips against his arm, and said, "Clint, that's—"

"I know who it is, Joy," he said. "Go over by the bar and stay with Frank. Tell him not to do anything stupid . . . until I do."

"But—"

"Do as I say, Joy," he snapped under his breath, "and don't run. Just walk over there and tell Frank what I said." He looked at her then and added, "Unless you want to run out the back way and tell Jory what's happening."

Her eyes widened at his words, but before she could say anything, Clint said, "Get going."

Clint kept his eyes on the big man as Joy made her way to the bar. He glanced over at Frank, who frowned as Joy relayed his message, then looked over at Clint and nodded slightly.

The two men with Saber broke off from behind him and walked over to the bar. Saber approached the poker game, and Clint knew he was going to take the lone empty seat and join the game. He also wondered how

173

Saber could be sure that the sheriff wasn't going to come along and interrupt things.

As Saber reached the game, Clint stretched his legs out and pushed his chair back a bit from the table. It was all going to boil down to this, he thought, and Jory is sitting home, relaxing, awaiting the outcome. *Let's just hope*, he thought, *that we can disappoint Mr. Sherman Jory . . .*

"Mind if I sit in?" Saber asked, resting his hand on the back of the empty chair.

A few of the players looked up and Clint saw that they recognized him. Whether or not it was from that night that Pop Cook was killed, he didn't know.

"Help yourself, friend," Clint said.

He dealt out the last card of the hand that was in progress, and bet ten dollars on his open pair of aces. Two players dropped and one called. Clint took the hand with aces over.

Depending on Leslie to watch the other two men, Clint kept his eyes on the table as he dealt out five hands of seven-card stud.

He figured Saber would find something wrong with his dealing in the first few hands, but he played for over an hour, and was actually ahead a few hundred before trouble started.

Saber had four clubs on the table, and everyone but the house had gone out, because he was betting like he already had the fifth in the hole. With the seventh and last card coming, Clint raised with a pair of deuces on the table.

"You're raising four open clubs?" Saber asked, matter-of-factly.

"With fifty dollars," Clint said.

"You're either very sure I don't have it, or very sure

I'm not going to get it," the big man said. "How could that be, Mister Dealer?"

"Play your cards," Clint advised him. "Call, raise or fold."

"I'll raise," Saber said, pushing a hundred dollars into the pot.

"Call," Clint said, pushing in the required amount. "Last card coming out."

He dealt the final card of the hand to each of them, then bet his open pair of deuces.

"Betting into my raise?" Saber asked. "You must have an awful lot of confidence in those deuces."

"I'm betting on all seven cards, mister, not just two deuces," Clint answered. "Play or fold."

"You're in control, aren't you?"

"The house usually is."

"Yeah, well maybe you're a little more in control. Maybe you know that I don't have a flush. Maybe you already know what I do have."

"I guess you're folding," Clint said. He put his cards down and reached for the pot with his left hand. As he figured, the saber came out and crashed down on the pot, just missing his hand.

"I'm not folding, Mister Dealer," Saber said. "You are."

"I just made a bet, friend," Clint reminded him. "If you don't call, and you don't raise, then you fold. That's the way the game is played."

"I'm making some new rules," Saber said in a low, menacing tone, and the other players at the table pushed back their chairs and fled from the table.

The entire saloon had gone quiet, and Clint hoped that Leslie had the other two men covered.

"What rules are those?" Clint asked.

"Cheaters lose," Saber said, and an audible intake of breath could be heard from several people in the room. Calling a man a cheater in a game of poker was tantamount to calling him out.

"Put up that saber," Clint said.

"Why?"

"Because if you don't I'll take it away from you."

The man's eyes flared with anger, and surprise.

"If you're thinking about busting this place up, forget it," Clint told him. "You did that once already."

"Then maybe I should just bust you up."

"Maybe you should try," Clint said, "but before you do, play your hand."

Saber stood up slowly, and Clint watched him closely. The man raised his saber off the pot, then turned his cards to reveal an ace high flush, which he'd made with the last card.

"Now yours," he told Clint.

The Gunsmith turned his cards to reveal the full house he'd had, three deuces over a pair of nines, before he'd even got the last card.

"You lose," he told the man called Saber.

"No," Saber replied. "you do."

He dropped the saber, and in that split second Clint knew that this was some kind of signal. Saber's right hand flashed for his gun and Clint saw it move, every inch of the way. As the man's hand touched his gun, Clint went for his, drew it smoothly and swiftly, clearing leather way before the other man did.

The Gunsmith fired and his bullet caught Saber high in his broad chest, knocking him back a few steps. At the same time, he became aware of other shots being fired. As Saber fell to the floor, his gun still leathered, the Gunsmith glanced over at the bar and saw Buckskin Frank Leslie with both Peacemakers out. The other two men who had come in with Saber were on the floor, dead.

Before either man could react, Martin Cort rushed into the room through the batwing doors, and was obviously surprised by what he saw.

"Saber—" he said, and then his eyes found the big man's form lying on the floor.

"Leather the gun, Cort," Clint said.

Cort took a couple of moments to assess the situation, then put up his gun. Leslie watched the Gunsmith leather his, and put away his own.

"Running in with your gun out, eh, Cort?" Clint said. "And looking for Saber. What were you supposed to do, shoot him in the back after he and his men killed us?" Cort's glance flicked nervously from Clint to Leslie and back to the Gunsmith. "Jory was going to clean it up all the way around, wasn't he? Only he wasn't going to stop with Saber."

"What do you mean?" Cort asked.

"He couldn't leave you around to talk, could he? You know too much, Cort."

"You're crazy. Jory doesn't have to kill me."

"Maybe not, but he's aiming too high to take a chance."

"Cort," Leslie said, coming around the bar. "You were going to backshoot Saber . . . the way you shot me in the back?"

"I should have shot straighter—" Cort growled before he realized what he was saying and stopped himself short.

"Well, now's your chance, big man," Leslie said. "You been pushing for this all along."

Cort looked over at Clint, who lifted his hands and said, "This is between you and Frank, Cort. Take your best shot."

Cort turned so that he was facing Frank Leslie full on, and Clint kept one eye on the action and one eye on the front doors, because he was sure that Jory had somebody set to come in and take care of Cort after he took care of Saber. The initial shooting was over, and when there was another shot or two, the assumption would have to be that Cort had run in and shot Saber, making a hero out of himself.

Jory's problem was that he had underestimated Frank Leslie's recuperative abilities, and overestimated Saber's abilities.

Clint watched as Frank Leslie waited patiently for the nervous Cort to make his move.

Before either man could move, Deputy Steve Owen came running in with his gun out.

"Cort!" he shouted. Martin Cort, confused now, turned to face the deputy. Owen triggered his gun once, twice, knocking Martin Cort back as Sheriff Tom Sideman came in behind Owen.

"What—" Cort stammered. He turned to look at Adams, and his eyes said that he understood.

And then he died.

"What the hell—" Sideman said, looking around, taking in the carnage. All of the customers had pressed together against one wall, and now that the shooting was apparently over they began to drift back towards the center of the room.

"Everybody stay put!" Sideman shouted.

Everyone froze, except for Clint Adams. He took a few steps forward until he was facing Owen, then he grabbed the man's gun hand and hit him in the face with his fist. Owen staggered back and fell into a table and some chairs, dropping his gun. He tried to regain his balance, reaching for the gun, but Clint stepped on the deputy's hand and said, "Don't."

"What the hell is going on?" Sideman demanded. "Adams, get off my deputy's hand."

"After I pick up his gun," Clint said. He did so, and then removed his foot from Owen's hand.

"Get up, Steve," Sideman said. "Adams, I want to know what happened here."

"What happened here, Sheriff, is that Sherman Jory pushed his hand, and lost."

"Jory?" Sideman asked, looking around.

"Oh, he's not here, Sheriff, but his representatives are. There," Clint said, pointing at Saber and his two men, "there"—pointing at Martin Cort—"and there," pointing at Steve Owen.

"You're crazy," Owen said.

"You'd better explain," Sideman said.

"Jory hired Saber and his men to kill Frank and me. After that was done, Cort was supposed to come in and kill Saber, because I'm sure Saber was the only one who knew who he was working for. After that, Jory had to get Cort out of the way, and that was to be done by your deputy."

"You don't know what you're talking about," Owen snapped.

"Look at Cort, Sheriff," Clint said. "Owen was so intent in killing him that he came running in with his gun out and fired before he realized that Cort's gun was in his holster."

Sideman took a step forward to check Cort's holster, then turned to his deputy and said, "His gun is in his holster. Why'd you shoot, Steve?"

"I—uh, I—"

"And why didn't you come over here an hour ago,"

Clint asked Sideman, "when Saber first walked in.
You've been looking for him, haven't you?"

"You know I have."

"Well, somebody must have recognized him when
he walked in. Somebody must have come over to your
office to tell you."

Sideman looked at Steve Owen, and then back to
Clint.

"I was taking a nap inside one of the cells," the
lawman said. "Steve was sitting in the office."

"No one came to the office, or I would have woke
you up, Sheriff," Owen insisted.

"That's not true, Sheriff," Frank Leslie said, speaking for the first time. Everyone looked over to the bar,
where Leslie was standing, leaning against it. "I sent
Sandy Stevens over to your office as soon as Saber
walked in."

"Is he here?"

Leslie started looking over the people who were
standing against the wall.

"Look, this is ridiculous," Steve Owen insisted.
"I'm sorry if Cort didn't have his gun out, but I thought
he did—"

"Come on, Steve," Clint said. "You're an experienced man. You know when a man is holding a gun and
when he isn't. How much did Jory offer you, Steve? It
must have been a lot."

"I didn't—"

"You can see how he works, though. He had Cort
ready to kill Saber, and you ready to kill Cort. How
long did you think you'd last?"

Owen started to reply, then looked down at the
bodies of Saber and Cort and started thinking.

"Look, Sheriff, I've got proof that Jory had been

using his position at the bank to take over businesses in this town.''

''That doesn't mean he hired these men to kill you,'' Sideman maintained.

''Sheriff,'' Frank Leslie said, ''Stevens doesn't seem to have come back. I guess he wanted to avoid the shooting.''

''I'm sure we'll be able to find him,'' Clint offered. ''What do you say, Steve? Shall we go and look for him?''

Owen studied the faces of the people who were watching him, then looked down at the dead bodies again.

''No,'' he said, finally, ''don't go looking for him. It's true. Jory bought me,'' he said bitterly, ''and I guess he did intend for me to end up like Saber and Cort.''

''And was probably going to do it himself,'' Clint added. ''You're probably saving your own life by talking, Steve.''

''And losing my job.''

''And a little more,'' Sideman added, taking the badge off of Owen's shirt.

''But then you did that when you accepted Jory's money,'' Clint reminded him.

Steve Owen laughed bitterly and said, ''I haven't even gotten paid yet.''

''That's not very smart business, Steve,'' Clint said. ''But maybe you can pay Jory back, anyway.''

''Yeah,'' Owen said, ''maybe I can.''

Chapter Forty-Five

When Clint Adams left Marley Jory's house two mornings later, he could not recall ever having spent a night quite like it before. With Sherman Jory in jail, put there by Steve Owen's confession and the papers supplied by Marley, there had been no danger of their being interrupted, so the Gunsmith's last night in Brightwater had been a memorable one.

He went to the Buckskin Saloon to say good-bye to Frank Leslie. He used his key to get in and then handed it over to Leslie, who was waiting for him with two cups of coffee.

"You can keep that," Leslie told him, "seeing as how you're still a silent partner."

"I won't need it, Frank," he replied. "Give it to Joy."

Frank Leslie and Joy Darling had come to an agreement, and she was to continue to work for him. Both he and Clint believed her when she told them that although she had been planted on them by Sherman Jory, she had never given him any information he could use.

Clint had a feeling that, before long, the relationship would become more than just business.

"You won't change your mind and stay?" Leslie asked him.

"I don't think so," Clint said. "I've got to be

moving on. Just make sure my share of the profits goes to that bank at the address I gave you."

Leslie nodded and said, "As long as there are profits."

"Oh, I think there'll be plenty. You've still got to make payments to the bank, of course, but without Jory pressuring you, you'll be paid up before long, and then it'll be all yours. Eventually you'll be able to hire a dealer, bring in some tables . . . You're going to do fine, Frank." Clint stood up and said, "Just fine."

Frank Leslie stood up and extended his hand, saying, "I appreciate all your help, Clint, and your friendship."

"Take care of yourself, and the place, Frank. Good luck."

Clint left, and walked over to the livery, where his rig and Duke were waiting for him, all set to go. There was someone else waiting for him as well.

Sheriff Tom Sideman.

"Getting ready to go, I see," Sideman said.

"That's right."

"I could use a deputy, you know."

"I know you could, but it won't be me." Clint took Duke's reins and tied him to the back of the wagon. "I took off my badge a long time ago, Sheriff, and for good reasons. It would take reasons just as good for me to put one back on."

"I understand." He watched Clint climb aboard his rig and then said, "Clint, I'm sorry I gave you such a hard time about Jory."

"That's okay, Sheriff," Clint assured him. "He looked respectable."

"Yeah, I guess looks really can be deceiving."

"Something good might have come out of all this, though, for you and the town."

"How's that? I'm still looking for a deputy."

"Everybody knows that Mayor Ellis and Jory were good friends," the Gunsmith reminded the lawman. "Come election time, I think the town will be looking for a new mayor." He picked up the reins and said, "After the election, maybe you'll be looking for a new sheriff, as well as a deputy. Good luck."

Clint drove his rig down Brightwater's main street so he could take one last look at the Buckskin Saloon. He was glad that Buckskin Frank Leslie had found a place where he could settle down, and maybe eventually he too would be able to trade in his guns for an apron—for good.

But for some reason, the Gunsmith didn't feel he'd ever get that lucky.

GREAT BOOKS

E-BOOKS

AUDIOBOOKS

& MORE

Visit us today

www.speakingvolumes.us